IN A FLASH THE
RATTLESNAKE COILED . . .

Acting on pure instinct, Nate grabbed at his pistols. His left moccasin stepped on a loose rock and he tripped, starting to fall backwards onto the very stones the rattler had been concealed under.

The venomous reptile's tail began to buzz loudly.

Nate came down hard on his back, wincing when the sharp edges of several jagged rocks lanced into his body. He pulled the pistols free and cocked them at the same instant the rattler struck.

The snake speared its head at his right foot.

As if in slow motion, Nate saw the rattler open its mouth, saw the snake's long, hooked fangs ready to tear into his skin, and he jerked his leg away from that deadly maw. He saw the reptile miss by the merest fraction, and then he had the pistols extended and pointed at the rattlesnake. His fingers tightened and both guns cracked and belched smoke. For several seconds he couldn't see the serpent.

Had he hit it?

Other books in the WILDERNESS series

KING OF THE MOUNTAIN

2:
WILDERNESS
Lure of the Wild

David Thompson

LEISURE BOOKS   NEW YORK CITY

Dedicated to . . .
Judy, Joshua, and Shane.

And to all those in the black powder fraternity who know that shooting a Hawken ranks right up there with wild onions and fresh venison.

A LEISURE BOOK®

November 1990

Published by

Dorchester Publishing Co., Inc.
276 Fifth Avenue
New York, NY 10001

Printed in the United States of America.

Chapter One

"Indians," the lead rider said softly.

Both men immediately reined up.

The second rider, the younger of the duo, sat anxiously astride his mare and took a firmer grip on the Hawken in his right hand. He scanned the surrounding forest, his keen eyes scouring every shadow and possible place of concealment, the northwesterly breeze stirring his long black hair. Like his companion, he wore buckskins. A knife with a 12-inch blade rested in a sheath on his left hip. Slanted across his broad chest were his powder horn and bullet pouch. Tucked under his belt were two pistols. "Where?" he asked.

"Over yonder," the first man said, and nodded at the mountain slope to the southwest. In contrast to his youthful companion, the lead rider sported shoulder-length hair, a beard, and a mustache that were all as white as the snow capping the towering peaks to their rear. His eyes were a striking sea blue. A brown beaver hat adorned his head, and cradled in his big arms was a Hawken.

"I don't see them," the younger man commented.

"Keep looking, Nate."

His eyes narrowing, Nate scrutinized the slope carefully, estimating they were at least a half mile from the mountain in question. Large boulders dotted the slope, interspersed with stands of evergreen trees, typical terrain for the west slope of the Rocky Mountains. "I still don't see any Indians, Shakespeare."

The older man chuckled. "You're just like your uncle was when he first came out to the Rockies, Nathaniel King. You're blind as a bat and have the ears of a worm."

"Worms don't have ears."

"You're learning."

Nate started to smile, but he froze when he detected movement on the mountain slope and spied the five Indians riding at a leisurely pace from west to east, apparently using a narrow trail running from the top of the mountain to the bottom.

"Don't move," Shakespeare advised. "They haven't seen us yet. If we're lucky, they won't." He paused. "Those Devils are Utes."

The name jarred Nate's memory. "My uncle told me the Utes kill every white man they come across."

"And Zeke was right."

"What do we do if they see us?"

"Tuck our tails between our legs and cut out."

His skin tingling, Nate watched the five Utes ride lower down the mountain. The distance was too great for him to distinguish the details of their dress and the weapons they carried, but he had no doubt that each warrior was well armed.

"They're probably heading over the Continental Divide to the Plains," Shakespeare mentioned. "Going to do a little buffalo hunting, or maybe raid the Cheyennes or the Arapahos."

"Will they use the same pass we did?"

"Most likely."

"Then they'll see our tracks in the snow."

"So? By the time the Utes reach that pass, we'll be long gone. And even if they do try to trail us, they won't follow us very far," Shakespeare predicted.

"Why not?" Nate asked.

"Because they're not stupid. They'll figure that we're white men because that horse you bought in New York is shod. Then they'll work it out in their heads that we must be heading for the rendezvous at Bear Lake."

"The Utes know about the rendezvous?"

Shakespeare snickered. "Every tribe in these parts knows about the get-together of all the trappers and the fur traders. A lot of the tribes sends groups to the rendezvous to trade, sell their women, and such."

"And the Utes won't follow us there?"

"No. For two very important reasons. First, they'd be shot on sight. Second, we'll be passing through the Green River country, and no Ute in his right mind wants to go there."

Nate saw the five Utes disappear behind a cluster of trees. "Why not?"

"Because the Blackfeet roam that area."

That name sparked another memory. Nate glanced at his companion. "Uncle Zeke told me that the Blackfeet are one tribe I should avoid at all costs."

"And Zeke spoke the truth, as always. The damn Blackfeet are the most warlike tribe west of the Mississippi. They fight everyone. Even the other tribes think they're war crazy and that says a lot because most tribes like going to war."

"They do?"

"Sure. Why, there's hardly three tribes in the whole Indian Country that are friendly to one another, except for the Cheyennes and the Arapahos. They just can't get along. And the Blackfeet are the most feared of the lot,"

Shakespeare disclosed.

"Have you ever run into them?" Nate inquired.

"A few times."

"What happened?"

"Let me put it this way. The Blackfoot warrior who hangs my scalp in his lodge will be the envy of the tribe."

Aligning his Hawken across his thighs, Nate surveyed the mountain slope. "I don't see the Utes."

"We can keep going," Shakespeare said, and rode onward. "I want to cover as much ground as we can today."

Nate followed. "How long will it take us to reach Bear Lake?"

"About a week, if we're lucky and push it. The rendez-vous will be in full swing when we get there. I'm taking the shortest route I know of. If we'd had the time to spare, I would have gone up the Sweetwater Valley and then over the Divide at South Pass. It's a lot easier that way, but we'd miss almost all of the rendezvous," Shakespeare detailed.

Nate glanced over his right shoulder at the rim of snow-covered peaks behind them, to the east. "What was the name of that pass we used?"

"It doesn't have a name. Not many folks know it exists. The Indians do, of course. You and me. And Zeke did."

The mention of his uncle brought a frown to Nate's face and he stared glumly at the terrain, thinking of the man who had lured him to the West under false pretenses, the man he had grown to care for as much as he did his own father. By all rights he should despise Zeke for the dirty trick he had played on him, but he couldn't bring himself to feel angry, not when the six weeks or so he had spent in Zeke's company had been the six happiest weeks of his entire life.

Nate shook his head in disbelief. Had it only been about

three months ago that he had departed New York City in response to the letter sent by Ezekiel? The time seemed longer. Much, much longer. So much had happened. He'd nearly been robbed and killed. He'd crossed the prairie in company with his uncle, surviving encounters with cutthroats, a grizzly bear, and a war party of Kiowas. He'd made it all the way to the uncharted vastness of the Rocky Mountains, to his uncle's cabin high up in the rugged wilderness, only to see his uncle slain at the hands of an avenging Kiowa warrior.

All that, and for what?

For a treasure that never existed, at least not in the way he had anticipated.

Zeke's letter had hinted at great riches. His uncle had extended an invitation to meet him in St. Louis, and promised to share "the greatest treasure in the world." Believing that Zeke had found gold or made a fortune in the fur trade, hoping to use his share of the wealth to woo his beloved Adeline Van Buren, Nate had decided to take Zeke up on the offer.

How was he to know the offer had been a sham?

Nate sighed and watched a squirrel scamper from branch to branch in a nearby tree. He'd traveled almost a thousand miles to St. Louis and met his uncle, only to have Zeke inform him that he must venture all the way to the Rocky Mountains if he wanted to see Zeke's "treasure." The prospect of being away from Adeline for a year had troubled Nate immensely, but he had justified going with Zeke on the pretext that the wealth he would obtain would make the separation and hardships entailed worthwhile.

But was that the real reason?

Quite often of late, Nate found himself speculating that there might be another, underlying reason why he had allowed himself to be duped. True, he'd genuinely liked Ezekiel. True, he had wanted to impress Adeline by acquiring riches beyond her wildest dreams. Also true, however, was the fact that he had been thrilled at having the opportunity to journey into a savage realm few white men had ever penetrated. In his youth he had read countless stories about the fierce Indians and the wild beasts inhabiting the unmapped lands beyond the frontier, and had often imagined the adventures he would have if he was to go west.

Now his dreams were coming true.

Nate's reflection was interrupted by a question from his companion.

"Did you bring that scalp along?"

The corners of Nate's mouth curled downward slightly as he thought of the Kiowa warrior he had slain, the Indian whose scalp he had taken to fulfill a promise made to his dying uncle. He glanced at the pack horse he was leading, at the blanket in which he had rolled up the scalp, then looked at Shakespeare. "I brought it."

"Good."

"What's good about it?"

"The Indians and quite a few of the whites out here place a lot of stock in taking the hair of an enemy. It marks you as a man."

"Have you taken any scalps?"

"Thirty-two."

The number staggered Nate. He'd taken the Kiowa warrior's hair in the heat of a burning rage over his uncle's death. Without that fury to act as a stimulus, he doubted whether he could have performed the grisly task. "I don't know if I can ever take another one," he commented.

"You will."

"How can you be so sure?"

"To be, or not to be. That's the question. Whether it's nobler in the mind to suffer the slings and arrows of outrageous fortune, or to take arms against a sea of troubles, and by opposing end them," the white-haired mountain man replied.

"Shakespeare again?"

"Sort of."

"Why do you like him so much? I struggled through some of his works in school, and I never could understand half of what I read."

"Old William S. was one of the wisest mothers' sons who ever lived. I picked up a book of his plays about thirty years ago, and I've been reading him ever since. It's gotten so that I'm a fair hand at quoting him. I reckon that's why everyone now calls me Shakespeare."

Nate stared at the roll tied behind Shakespeare's saddle, where the frontiersman kept his book on the English playright, and thought of his own affinity for the works of James Fenimore Cooper. "What's your real name?"

Shakespeare unexpectedly halted and twisted. "Let me give you a word of advice, Nate. You're the nephew of the best friend I ever had, and I've made it my business to teach you how to survive out here. One thing you must never do is pry into another man's personal affairs. If a man volunteers information about himself, about his past or whatever, all well and good. But don't go poking your nose in where it doesn't belong or someone is likely to try and shoot it off."

"All I did was ask your name," Note noted defensively.

"And if I ever figure I can trust you enough, I'll tell you my name," Shakespeare said.

Nate's forehead furrowed in confusion as he mulled the implications of the other man's remarks. What possible motive could Shakespeare have for not revealing his own name? Was he embarrassed by it, as some people occasionally were? Or could there be a darker motive? Was Shakespeare wanted by the authorities somewhere? Did the mountain man have an evil secret buried somewhere in his past he wanted no one to know? "Sorry I asked," he commented. "I meant no offense."

"None taken," Shakespeare said, and resumed riding in a northwesterly direction.

Nate lapsed into silence, mentally debating whether he had made another mistake by deciding to remain in the West for a spell instead of returning to the States. After Zeke had died, he'd spent a sleepless night sitting out under the star-filled firmament, pondering the course he should take, weighing the pros and cons, trying to gauge the consequences of both options.

One factor had stood out above the others. He had informed Adeline that he would be acquiring great wealth. In the letter he'd composed to her before leaving New York City, and again in the epistle he'd sent from St. Louis, he'd related Zeke's pledge to share the "treasure" and promised to return to New York incredibly rich. What would Adeline think when she learned the truth? How would she react when she discovered he had been duped? How would she feel towards him when she found out there never had been any gold or silver or money garnered in the lucrative fur trade? Would she think him a fool, or worse?

He couldn't blame her if she did.

How was he to know that Ezekiel King's treasure wasn't anything material, wasn't anything he could hold in his hands or hoard at the bank? He could still vividly remember the earnest expression on his uncle's face as Zeke lay dying, and the words Zeke spoke that seared into his brain and struck a responsive chord.

"Take a good look at this valley, Nate," Zeke had said. "Look at the wildlife, at the deer and the elk and the other game. Think about the fact that all this is now yours. My cabin, my rifle, my clothes, everything I leave to you. And I leave you with one more thing. The greatest treasure in the world. The treasure that I found when I came out to the Rockies. The treasure I wanted to share with the only relative I give a damn about. The treasure I wanted to share with you, Nate.''

''What treasure?'' Nate had asked.

''Freedom.''

The one word had provoked a peculiar response. Nate had later gazed at the majestic mountain peaks ringing the valley, at the abundant wildlife, at a sparkling lake situated not far from his uncle's cabin, a lake swarming with ducks and geese and fowl of every description; he had stared overhead at the brilliant blue sky, and inhaled the crisp, invigorating high-altitude air; and for a brief, insightful moment, a few seconds of lucid contemplation, he had actually felt that distinctive, transcendent freedom his uncle had alluded to, the pure, pristine freedom of a soul unfettered by the restraints of civilization.

Nate cherished that feeling, an exquisite sensation he had never known before. How could he return to New York now, after tasting a morsel of genuine freedom? New more importantly, how could he return to Adeline without the wealth he had promised? How could he go back a failure? Both reasons for remaining in the Rockies vied with one another for dominance, and he had yet to resolve his true motivation for staying and for deciding to go to the rendezvous. He had—

''It appears I've miscalculated a mite,'' Shakespeare intruded on Nate's rumination.

''How so?''

Shakespeare pointed to the southwest. ''Here come the Utes.''

Chapter Two

Nate shifted and glanced to the left, and there were the five Ute warriors bearing down on them at breakneck speed. Even as he spied them, his eyes widening in alarm, they uttered loud war whoops and one of them foolishly snapped off a rifle shot.

"Stay close!" Shakespeare bellowed, and took off to the right, angling across the narrow valley they had been following, his white horse throwing up clods of earth with its hooves.

Expecting to feel an arrow penetrate his back at any moment, Nate kept as close to Shakespeare as he could, his mare pounding under him, the pack horse only a few feet to the rear of his mount.

The piercing shrieks of the Utes rose in volume.

They're gaining! Nate realized, and swallowed hard. He saw that his companion was making for a stand of trees several hundred yards off, and he risked a hasty look over his left shoulder to determine the position of the warriors.

Riding as if they were born on the back of a horse, their animals flying over the ground, the Utes were approximately five hundred yards to the southwest, waving their weapons and bellowing in anticipation of slaying the intruders into their territory.

Nate rode as he had never ridden before, his body rising and falling with the rhythm of his mare, his left hand holding the reins, his right hand clutching the Hawken and the lead to the pack animal, his blood coursing through his body even faster than the mare was running. He concentrated on the stand of trees, struggling to suppress the panic welling within him, knowing if he lost his head he would lose his life.

The Utes whooped and hollered, giving the impression there were scores of them instead of only five.

Shakespeare glanced back once, a devilish grin creasing his visage.

What did he find so humorous? Nate wondered, licking his dry lips, remembering how his Uncle Zeke had demonstrated the same peculiar, lighthearted attitude when confronted with danger, as if a life-and-death situation were a mere game of some sort. He doubted if he would ever understand these rugged, individualistic men who inhabited the unknown regions of the West. They seemed to possess an outlook on life that differed greatly from their cultured cousins in the States.

For a tense minute the race continued, the Utes doing their utmost to close on their quarry before the mountain men could reach the trees, but they were still a hundred yards away when the white-haired man reached the stand, practically leaped from his horse, and whirled.

Nate saw Shakespeare whip the Hawken up and fire, apparently without taking deliberate aim, and yet when Nate glanced back he beheld one of the Utes pitching to the ground.

Shakespeare voiced a whoop at his own.

And now Nate smiled as he reined up and vaulted to Shakespeare's side. ''Nice shooting,'' he commented, keeping his voice as calm as he could. He raised his Hawken and took careful aim, not wanting to waste the shot, sighting on the Indian riding on the right, scarcely breathing. He waited several seconds to be certain, then fired.

Eighty yards out the Ute threw his arms in the air and toppled backwards.

"We'll teach those savages a thing or two," Shakespeare remarked, in the process of reloading, his practiced fingers performing the task with astonishing speed.

Nate began to reload his rifle.

The three remaining Utes were still coming on strong. One of them unleashed an arrow.

"Watch out!" Shakespeare warned, and gave Nate a shove.

Startled, Nate looked up in time to see the arrow hurtling out of the blue. The shaft whizzed through the air and thudded into the ground at the exact spot where he had been standing.

"Quills are for porcupines," Shakespeare quipped, and aimed at the Ute with the bow. An instant later his rifle cracked and belched a ball and smoke.

The bow-wielder was in the act of drawing back the buffalo-sinew string when the shot hit him high on the chest and flung him over his mount's rump. In concert the remaining pair of warriors swung to the left, hunching low, glaring at the whites, racing for cover.

Nate finished reloading and lifted the Hawken to fire again.

"Don't bother," Shakespeare advised, watching the Utes depart. "We don't want to kill them all."

"We don't?" Nate declared in astonishment. "But they were trying to kill us."

Shakespeare glanced at the younger man and chuckled.

"Bloodthirsty son of a gun, aren't you? No, we don't want to kill all of them and I'll tell you why." He paused and stared at the fleeing Indians. "Out here, Nate, a man's reputation is as important as the man himself. Those two will go back to their tribe and report that they tried to take the hair of old Carcajou and failed. They'll embellish the story a bit, and make me out to be a fire-breathing demon who can down an enemy at a thousand yards. Now that will add considerably to my reputation, and the next time some Utes stumble across me they'll likely think twice before attempting to take my hair. Understand?"

"I believe so," Nate said. He observed the Utes vanish in the forest. "What was that name you mentioned? Carcajou?"

Shakespeare nodded. "If you live out here long enough, and if you become acquainted with the friendly Indians, you might acquire an Indian name of your own. Long ago the Flatheads gave me the name Carcajou."

"What does it mean?"

"It's another name for the wolverine."

"What's a wolverine?"

The frontiersman looked at Nate and laughed. "You'll learn soon enough."

Puzzled by the answer, Nate cradled his rifle. "I already have an Indian name of my own," he mentioned.

"You do?" Shakespeare responded in surprise.

"Yes. A Cheyenne named White Eagle gave it to me."

"I know him. He's a member of their Bow String Society."

"Their what?"

Shakespeare chortled. "You have so much to learn, it's pitiful. Most of the tribes living on the Plains have what they call soldier or warrior societies. They're a lot like those fancy, exclusive clubs for the rich back in the States, only the soldier societies have as their members the bravest men, the best fighters. The Cheyennes, as I recollect, have six societies.'' He paused, then began counting them off on his fingers. ''The Bow String, the Crazy Dogs, the Red Shields, the Fox Soldiers, the Elk Soldiers, and the Dog Soldiers.''

''So White Eagle must be an important man in their tribe?'' Nate inquired.

''I'll say. He's one of their top war chiefs.''

The news staggered Nate. He recalled the first time he'd seen White Eagle, shortly after being mauled by the grizzly that had surprised him when he wasn't carrying his rifle. He'd managed to plunge his butcher knife into the bear's head, and his uncle had finished the bruin off with a well-placed shot from a Hawken.

Later, during the battle with the Kiowas war party, White Eagle and other Cheyennes had arrived and rendered assistance. Before riding off, White Eagle had bestowed a gift and the name on Nate, and only now was he truly beginning to appreciate the significance of both acts. ''I had no idea,'' he mumbled.

''What name did White Eagle give you?'' Shakespeare asked.

''Grizzly Killer.''

The corners of Shakespeare's mouth started to curl upward, and he looked as if he was about to burst out laughing. He scrutinized Nate for a moment, then suddenly sobered. ''You're not pulling my leg?''

''Nope.''

''Well, I'll be,'' Shakespeare said, his brow knitting. ''A true knight, not yet mature, yet matchless, firm of word, speaking in deeds and deedless in his tongue, not soon provoked nor being provoked soon calmed, his heart and hand both open and both free.''

''What?''

''Never mind,'' Shakespeare replied. He scanned the

distant trees, ensuring the Utes were indeed gone.

"White Eagle also gave me an eagle feather," Nate mentioned.

"Where is it?"

"In my pack."

Shakespeare regarded his companion carefully. "Why aren't you wearing it?"

"I removed the feather from my hair after the first day because I couldn't sleep with it tied behind my head," Nate explained. "I haven't worn the thing since."

"I'm not one to offer advice unless asked, but if I were you I'd consider wearing the feather. They're marks of distinction for an Indian, and in some tribes you can't wear one unless you've killed an enemy," Shakespeare commented, his eyes narrowing. "Who did White Eagle see you kill?"

"A Kiowa warrior."

Shakespeare nodded. "White Eagle must regard you highly. If you're ever in Cheyenne country again, you'd best wear that feather. If you bump into him and you're not wearing it, he'll be offended."

"I'll keep that in mind," Nate promised. He glanced down at the arrow imbedded in the earth and bent over to pull the shaft out. "Another second and I'd have been a goner," he commented.

"Never underestimate an Indian with a bow," Shakespeare admonished. "They learn to shoot while standing, running, or from horseback when they're young boys, and they're accurate at over a hundred yards."

Nate studied the shaft thoughtfully.

"Not only that," Shakespeare went on, "they can fire arrows faster than you or I can load and fire a rifle. I saw a contest once between a trapper, a fellow who could shoot an acorn off a limb at fifty yards, and a Crow warrior. In the time it took the trapper to fire, reload, and fire again, that Crow got off twenty arrows.''

"Twenty?'' Nate repeated skeptically.

Shakespeare nodded. "And about ten years ago I spent some time in a Mandan village. The Mandans had this game they played, where the warriors tried to see which one of them could keep the most arrows in the air at the same time. Their best bowman, the best damn archer I ever saw, could keep nine arrows in the air all at once.''

Nate whistled. The more he learned about the prowess of the Indians, the more amazed he became that any white men managed to survive in the wilderness.

"Let's mount up and skedaddle,'' Shakespeare suggested. He walked to his horse, which stood patiently nibbling at grass several yards away.

"You're certain those Utes won't try to circle around and ambush us?'' Nate asked, moving toward his mare.

"As certain as I was they hadn't spotted us earlier,'' Shakespeare said, and laughed.

"Well, now I'm relieved,'' Nate quipped.

Minutes later they were mounted and riding to the northwest across an open, grassy expanse stretching to more mountains ten miles away.

"Let this incident be a lesson to you,'' Shakespeare said after they had traveled a quarter of a mile without seeing any sign of the Utes.

"Let me guess. I should never turn my back on an Ute.''

"No. You should always trust your own instincts, no matter what someone else with more experience might tell you. Go with your gut, as I like to say. My gut has saved my hide more times than I care to recollect.''

"But your instincts didn't warn you about those Utes,'' Nate noted.

Shakespeare chuckled. "Which brings to mind another saying I'm fond of. Most folks have no more brains in their head than they do in their elbow.''

"I like that," Nate said cheerfully, beginning to relax, already filing the fight with the Utes in the back of his mind as just another wilderness memory.

"That saying is taken straight from old William S."

"You're kidding me?"

"Nope. *Troilus and Cressida.* Act Two, Scene One."

Nate shook his head in astonishment. "You sure know your Shakespeare."

"I guess I do. Who would ever have figured I'd acquire such a classical education in the Rocky Mountain College."

"The what?"

"The Rocky Mountain College. That's the term us mountain folk use to describe all those long winter nights when it's too cold to trap and we're sitting around the fire in our toasty lodge debating everything under the sun."

"Zeke didn't tell me about it."

"Your uncle didn't have time to tell you about every aspect of life out here before he died. Give yourself a while. In a few years you won't be a greenhorn any longer."

"I don't know if I'll stay out here that long," Nate confided.

"You will."

"How can you be so certain?"

"You're a King."

"So? I have brothers back in the States who will never venture out of New York."

Shakespeare glanced at Nate. "You're different. You're like your uncle was, filled with the urge to roam, to see new lands and have adventures. That's what brought me out here ages ago."

"Ages?"

"It seems that long, sometimes," Shakespeare said wistfully. "The years are longer when you cram them with experience, when you live life to the fullest like the Good Lord intended. In the States, especially in the cities, most people go from day to day doing exactly the same thing they did the day before. They get up at the same time every morning, go to the same job each day, come home to the same house at night, and sleep in the same bed under the same covers. Their lives streak past like a shooting star, and before they know it someone is dropping dirt on their coffin and they haven't experienced one damn thing life has to offer."

"I never thought of it that way."

"You'll see. In a year from now you'll agree with me."

Nate thought of the Utes, the Blackfeet, and the Kiowas. "If I live that long."

Chapter Three

Several days later, after crossing another mountain range, they came to a remarkable expanse of arid, steep canyons totally different from the Rockies. Columns of red sandstone reared everywhere. Game became scarce and vegetation virtually nonexistent.

Nate took advantage of the trip to pepper Shakespeare with countless questions concerning the wildlife, the Indians, the general known geography of the land west of the Mississippi, and any other subject he could think of, adding substantially to the lore he had learned from Zeke. The aged frontiersman was a virtual fount of knowledge and wisdom, and Nate soaked up the information like a human sponge.

Shakespeare continued in a northwesterly direction, pushing their mounts as hard as he dared, eager to reach the rendezvous.

Nate found the older man's uncharacteristic hurry amusing. In every other aspect to Shakespeare's life, the man never displayed the slightest inclination to rush, but he was bound and determined to reach the annual gathering of trappers, traders, and friendly Indians while it was still in progress.

On the third day after the incident with the Utes, Shakespeare called a midday halt at a spring situated at the base of a steep plateau. They watered their animals and sat down to enjoy strips of jerked venison.

"Do you realize that not five white men in the whole world have been within ten miles of this spot?" Shakespeare asked. He took a bite of jerky and chewed vigorously.

"Really?" Nate responded absently, gazing out over the barren terrain.

"Prime beaver country is north of here. Few trappers ever bother to pass through this region because it's a waste of their time."

"Reminds me of a desert."

Shakespeare snorted. "If you want to see a real desert, you should travel into the territory west of the Great Salt Lake. There isn't a drop of water to be had anywhere, and your throat becomes so parched you drink your own sweat just to survive."

"You've been there?" Nate inquired.

"A few times."

"Is there any part of the land between the Mississippi and the Pacific you haven't seen?"

"There's more country I haven't seen than country I have," Shakespeare said. "And some of the parts I have laid eyes on were downright amazing."

"For instance?"

Shakespeare tilted his head and pondered for a full ten seconds. "Well, the most amazing wonders of all are located north of here a ways. There are boiling mud holes, geysers that shoot hundreds of feet in the air, and natural hot springs where the water is hot enough to scald you."

"Boiling mud holes?" Nate repeated skeptically. "Geysers?"

"Don't you believe me?"

"Of course. I know you're not one to invent tall tales. But still, boiling mud holes, you must admit, seem a little preposterous. I hope I see them myself, one day."

The frontiersman regarded the younger man for a minute, then broke into a grin and nodded. "Yep. If I hadn't of seen those geysers and mud holes, I'd probably say the same thing. I hope you do get to see them, Nate. If the land gets into your blood, you will."

"Into my blood?"

Shakespeare gestured at the far horizon. "The wilderness has a way of growing on a man. Those who come out west intending to spend a year or so trapping wind up staying four or five years. Some stay longer. Once you start traveling and beholding all the marvels, once you can live off the land like an Indian, and once you realize that life in the States is akin to being penned in a cage, you can't leave." He chuckled. "Once you've tasted genuine freedom, it's a mite hard to settle for anything less."

"There's that word again," Nate commented.

"Which word?"

"Freedom. Uncle Zeke said practically the same thing."

"He knew what he was talking about. Out here, where you don't have to answer to anyone, where you don't have taxes to pay or the government breathing down your back, where you don't have politicians trying to tell you how to live, is where you find the freedom our forefathers fought and died for."

"I didn't realize you're so political-minded," Nate said.

Shakespeare's eyes narrowed. "Don't you ever insult me like that again. Implying a man is like a politician is as bad as calling him a liar and a thief. There's hardly a politician alive worth his salt, and rare are those who knowing the true meaning of the word honor." He paused.

"Mine honor keeps the weather of my fate: Life every man holds dear, but the dear man holds honor far more precious-dear than life."

"Let me guess. More of your William S."

Shakespeare nodded. "I don't give a tinker's damn about politics, Nate, except when some dignified, vote-begging leach tries to take my freedom away. Then I can get riled."

"I've never paid much attention to politics," Nate mentioned.

"Good. Don't. The more you think about it, the more agitated you'll become," Shakespeare predicted. He placed his hands on the hard ground and pushed to his feet.

"Going somewhere?"

"Nature calls. I'll be back in a bit."

Nate watched his companion walk to a cluster of huge boulders to the south. Moments later Shakespeare disappeared among the rocks. He squinted up at the bright sun, then stood and stretched. After all that riding a little exercise seemed to be in order. He turned and strolled casually along the edge of the spring, gazing idly into the crystal-clear water while finishing his dried venison.

How strange fate could be.

Who would ever have thought that one day he would be standing next to a spring in the heart of an unexplored wildnerness? Or that he would be traveling with an old man who was as tough as leather and who could quote Shakespeare by the hour?

Nate grinned.

Who would ever have thought that he would have the courage to leave New York City and venture into the Great West? Who would ever have guessed that in the breast of an accountant lurked the heart of an adventurer? Which brought a pertinent question to mind. How far was he willing to go, both physically and personally? How much longer would he remain in the wilderness? What about beautiful Adeline, awaiting his return? How long could he reasonably expect her to wait for him? He'd told her in his letter from St. Louis that he would be gone about a year. Did she possess the patience to hold out for a year? Or would she grow lonely and bored and seek out other male suitors?

The realizataion sobered him.

He had to face facts. Adeline could have her pick of practically any man in New York. In the States, for that matter. And he wouldn't be justified in blaming her if she did acquire a new beau, not after he had up and left her without more than a day's notice.

What had he done?

Upset by his train of thought, Nate stopped and licked his dry lips. The water beckoned, and he knelt and dipped his right hand in the cool liquid. That jerked meat had made him extremely thirsty. Eager to drink, he flattened on his stomach and touched his mouth to the spring.

A strange rattling noise arose on his right.

Nate took a sip, puzzled by the rattling. He glanced at a pile of fair-sized stones within inches of his right arm, and froze.

Lying coiled under a large flat stone, its stout body tensed and ready to spring, its wide head hovering motion-less, its eerie eyes with their vertical pupils fixed on his neck, was an enormous rattlesnake.

Petrified, Nate didn't move a muscle. He scarcely breathed, his gaze riveted on those alien, wicked eyes. What should he do? Would the rattlesnake strike if he tried to rise and flee? Would the reptile slither away if he simply stayed glued to that spot?

The rattling continued unabated and the snake remained coiled, its long, forked black tongue flicking out and in.

Nate's initial panic began to subside. He concentrated

on keeping perfectly still. Sooner or later, he hoped, the reptile would leave. He'd heard somewhere, probably in school many years ago, that a rattlesnake wouldn't strike unless directly threatened, and he had no intention of posing the slightest possible threat.

A minute elapsed.

Two.

Sweat formed on Nate's brow and trickled down his back. He ignored the sensation. Don't move! he told himself over and over. Don't twitch a muscle!

The peculiar buzzing from the snake's rattles abruptly ceased.

Nate almost forgot himself, almost smiled in triumph. The rattler must be about to slide off to hunt or return to whatever hole it used as a den. He saw the reptile begin to glide forward. Elated, he watched the rattlesnake carefully, expecting it to turn to the left, away from the spring.

Instead, to his utter horror, the rattler came straight toward him!

Nate's terror returned in a rush, and only with a supreme effort could he prevent himself from trembling. The rattlesnake angled at his head, and for a heart stopping instant he thought it would bite his face. But the reptile slid up and over his neck, moving slowly, its cool scales rubbing against his flesh.

Dear God!

Nate wanted to scream. He gritted his teeth until they hurt and clenched his fists, wishing the rattler would pass completely over him quickly and go on its way.

The snake unexpectedly stopped.

No! No! No! Nate shrieked in his mind. Keep going! He could feel the weight of the reptile on his neck. The strain on his nerves was tremendous. What was it doing? Why had it stopped? He detected a flickering motion out of the corner of his left eye, and without moving his head he swiveled his eyes and caught sight of the cause.

The rattlesnake had turned. Its squat head was now near the water, its tongue continuing to dart out and back again.

What was it *doing*? Nate nearly bolted, but he willed himself to relax, to remain calm, certain the reptile would leave soon. The seconds dragged by. Beads of sweat dribbled down his cheeks and dripped from his chin. The pistols were gouging him in the abdomen. If only he dared make a grab for them!

A second later the rattler began to move away, its head weaving from side to side.

Nate felt the scales scraping his skin.

In another few seconds the snake would be gone!

A tingling sensation suddenly developed in Nate's nostrils and he experienced an urge to sneeze. Not now! He wiggled his nose, trying to suppress the impulse, to no avail. The tingling grew more intense. He went to lift his right hand, to clamp his fingers on his nostrils, but he was too late.

The sneeze, to his agitated mind, sounded like a gunshot.

Nate tensed and glanced at the rattlesnake, his blood racing when he saw the reptile snap around and stare directly at him. He expected to hear the rattling again, but the snake was motionless except for the constant flicking of its forked tongue.

What *now*?

Had the rattler realized he wasn't a log or a rock? Would it strike without warning? A quick roll to the left might enable him to escape. It also might trigger an attack. So his best bet appeared to be to stay still and do nothing.

The snake, apparently, had other ideas.

It started to crawl toward him.

Nate's eyes inadvertently widened and his breath caught in his throat. If the rattler sank its fangs into his face, he'd be a goner within minutes.

The rattlesnake glided slowly nearer.

Goose bumps erupted all over Nate's body. He watched the reptile draw to within six inches of his face, then stop, and he became acutely conscious of the rattler's eyes boring into his own. It knew! It knew he was something alive! Perhaps the snake was puzzled because he hadn't moved. Another thought occurred to him.

Maybe the rattlesnake was sizing him up before striking.

Nate decided he couldn't afford to lie still any longer. The rattler wasn't coiled, which should give him a few seonds of precious time to get out of the way before it could attack. Unless the rattlesnake didn't *need* to coil before launching itself, in which case he would be dead soon and Shakespeare would bury him just as he'd buried his uncle.

Shakespeare!

Where *was* he?

The rattler edged forward again.

Nate felt something rough pass over his neck and then the weight of the snake was gone. Unable to endure another moment of suspense, his nerves stretched to the breaking point, he uttered an inarticulate bellow and shoved upward, scrambling away from the reptile as he moved.

In a flash the rattlesnake coiled.

Acting on pure instinct, Nate grabbed at his pistols. His left moccasin stepped on a loose rock and he tripped, starting to fall backwards onto the very stones the rattler had been concealed under.

The venomous reptile's tail began to buzz loudly.

Nate came down hard on his back, wincing when the sharp edges of several jagged rocks lanced into his body. He pulled the pistols free and cocked them at the same instant the rattler struck.

The snake speared its head at his right foot.

As if in slow motion, Nate saw the rattler open its mouth, saw the snake's long, hooked fangs ready to tear into his skin, and he jerked his leg away from the deadly maw. He saw the reptile miss by the merest fraction, and then he had the pistols extended and pointed at the rattlesnake. His fingers tightened and both guns cracked and belched smoke. For several anxious seconds he couldn't see the serpent.

Had he hit it?

He listened for the buzzing, but the rattles were no longer shaking. Bracing his elbows against the rocks, he rose to a sitting posture and peered intently at the last spot where the snake had been.

The breeze dispersed the smoke.

And there lay the snake, its head severed from its body, the tongue jutting from its thin lips, those unnatural orbs still fixed in his direction.

Nate slowly stood, feeling suddenly limp. That had been too close for comfort! He licked his lips and took a step, then became aware of someone standing off to his left. Startled, he spun.

"Not bad," Shakespeare commented, his arms folded across his chest. "I couldn't have done better myself."

"How long have you been there?"

"A few minutes."

"A few minutes!" Nate snapped angrily. "Why didn't you do something?"

"What could I do? That snake was too close to you for me to risk a shot."

"You could have tried!" Nate declared.

"And deprive you of that valuable experience? I should say not," Shakespeare said, clucking his tongue. He strolled over to the rattler.

Nate wasn't certain he'd heard correctly. "Experience?

I was almost killed.''

The frontiersman turned a kindly gaze on his protégé. ''You have a lot to learn about life in the wilderness, Nate. The best teacher I know of is experience.'' He nodded at the reptile. ''Now you have experience with rattle-snakes.''

''But I could have been killed!'' Nate reiterated.

''No one ever claimed the lessons you have to learn would be easy.''

Nate glanced at the snake's head and inadvertently shuddered, his indignation beginning to dissipate.

''No hard feelings?'' Shakespeare asked.

''I guess not.''

''Good.''

''I'm just glad I already have experience with grizzlies.''

Chapter Four

Over the next few days they continued on their northwesterly course. They left the barren canyons far behind and entered country where the mountains were covered with thick stands of pine and the valleys were verdant. Game abounded. Buffalo, elk, deer, and antelope were everywhere. Bighorn sheep were visible on the higher rocky peaks. Eagle and hawks soared on the air currents.

Nate gradually forgave Shakespeare for the rattlesnake incident, but he vowed to keep a watchful eye on his companion in the future. If the older man had it in his head to teach a few more lessons, there was no telling what might be in store.

They were crossing a low knoll one afternoon when Shakespeare made an announcement. "We'll be at the rendezvous the day after tomorrow."

"I'm looking forward to it."

"Are you?"

Nate's eyes narrowed at the peculiar tone Shakespeare used. "Shouldn't I be?"

"Just be on your guard."

"Why? What could happen to me?"

"If you're not careful, I could be riding back alone."

"You're kidding me," Nate declared.

"Am I?"

"Quit talking in riddles."

"Fair enough," Shakespeare said, watching a raven wing to the north and listening to the swishing beat of its flapping wings. "Any old hand at the rendezvous will mark you as a greenhorn the moment they lay eyes on you. Most of the men will accept you and leave you alone. But there are a few troublemakers who may take it into their heads to test you."

"Test me?"

"Test your mettle. See if they can rile you. If they find they can get your goat just once, you won't know a minute's peace."

"Their behavior sounds childish to me," Nate commented.

Shakespeare grinned. "If you're going to survive the rendezvous, I'd better fill you in on what to expect." He paused. "To understand the goings on, you have to understand more about the life of a trapper. For an entire year these men are roaming the West, traveling from stream to stream, catching as many beaver as they can and getting their peltries ready for the annual get-together. Except for those who take up with a squaw, they live a pretty lonely life. They work from dawn to dusk every day when the weather permits, and you don't know what real work is until you spend most of the day working a trap line in ice-cold water and lugging around beaver that can weigh up to sixty pounds until you skin them."

Nate listened attentively.

"A trapper has to always be on the watch for hostiles. If caught, he'll be subjected to indescribable tortures. Things like having his ears and nose cut off, or his privates. Or maybe he'll be scalped and stuck in the ground up to his neck for the animals to finish off.''

Imagining the fate of such a hapless man, Nate grimaced.

"And if the Indians aren't enough to worry about, there are always the grizzlies. They've torn many a trapper up beyond recognition and left him to bleed to death. Then there's the chance of being caught in a flood or a snow-slide.''

"It sounds like a dangerous life," Nate acknowledged.

Shakespeare snorted. "Now there's an understatement if ever I heard one. Did you know that a couple of years ago over one hundred trappers left Santa Fe to spend a year in the mountains, and only sixteen made it back?''

"Sixteen?" Nate repeated in surprise.

"So now you have some idea of the life a trapper leads. And you can see how much they look forward to the rendezvous. After a year of doing without, a year of facing hardship after hardship, they're definitely ready to celebrate. To tell you the truth, most of them live for the few weeks each summer when they can drink and brawl and brag to their heart's content," Shakespeare related.

"How many of these rendezvous have you been to?''

"Three.''

"That's all?''

"There's only *been* three.''

"Oh.''

"A gent by the name of Ashley started them back in '25. The first one was at Henry's Fork on the Green River. In '26 it was held at Cache Valley. Last year was at Bear Lake, the same as this year.''

"How many trappers will be there?" Nate inquired.

"Depends. Somewhere between one and two hundred.''

Nate blinked a few times. "Two hundred?''

"And that doesn't count the breeds—''

"Breeds?" Nate interrupted.

The aged mountain man sighed. "Half-breeds. Born of white and Indian parents. I feel sorry for most of them."

"Why?"

"Because both the whites and the Indians tend to look down their noses at the mongrels. The breeds know better than to try and mingle in polite white society, and most of the tribes don't treat them much better."

"That's not fair."

"How green you are and fresh in this old world," Shakespeare quoted. "Who ever claimed life is fair? Is it fair for a fawn to be torn to pieces by a pack of starving wolves? Is it fair for trappers to be caught and mutilated by the Blackfeet? Is it fair for the owners of the fur-trading companies to get rich off the sweat and labor of honest trappers?"

Nate said nothing.

"Life is seldom fair," Shakespeare stressed. "Now where was I? Oh, yes. There might be upwards of two hundred trappers at the rendezvous, half as many breeds, and a goodly amount of Indians. The Snakes, the Flatheads, the Nez Perce, the Crows, and the Bannocks will likely show up. Maybe a couple of thousand, all told."

"I had no idea."

"What did you expect? A dozen old farts sitting around telling tall tales about their adventures in the Rockies?"

"No," Nate said defensively.

"Keep your eyes and ears open at the rendezvous and you'll learn more in a couple of weeks about life out here than I could teach you in a month."

"I will."

They rode in silence for over five miles, paralleling a stream winding through a wide valley.

"Can I ask you a question?" Nate inquired.

"Go ahead."

"It might be too personal."

"Don't worry. I'm not about to shoot you for prying into my personal life," Shakespeare said, and grinned.

"Have you ever bought an Indian woman?"

Shakespeare glanced at the younger man, his brow furrowed. "That bothers you, does it?"

"A little," Nate conceded.

"Why?"

"I regard buying an Indian woman the same as buying a Negro slave. You might have heard that the state of New York abolished slavery last year. There are a lot of people back in the East who consider slavery an abomination. The minister at our church called slavery a moral and spiritual evil."

"Do tell."

"That's right. I just don't think it's decent to treat another human being like a piece of property."

"Correct me if I'm wrong, but aren't most of those Negroes brought to the States on ships from some far-off country like Africa?"

"Yes," Nate answered.

"And the Negroes are brought over whether they want to come or not?"

"That's what everyone says."

Shakespeare nodded. "I thought so. To you the practice might appear the same, but there's a world of difference between buying an Indian woman and buying a Negro slave."

"In what respect?"

"For one thing, most of the time the Indian women want to be bought."

"They do?" Nate queried skeptically.

"The height of any Indian woman's ambition is to get herself married off, and to the Indians buying a woman is the same as marrying her off. You get all upset at the notion of white men purchasing an Indian girl. I'll bet you don't even know that Indian men do the same thing.''

"I didn't know.''

"There. See? Ignorance is its own worst enemy. Yes, Indian men buy their wives. The usual way is for the warrior to offer a certain number of good horses, and maybe other items besides. Let's say, for instance, that a Sioux warrior has his sights set on a pretty girl. He sends the horses to her lodge and has a friend or a relative announce his intention to marry her. If she accepts the horses, then they hold a big feast in a day or so and the marriage is sealed,'' Shakespeare detailed.

"And all the Indian men pay for the brides?'' Nate inquired.

"Pretty near. So is it any wonder the white men do the same? If a white man tried to marry an Indian woman without purchasing her, there'd be hell to pay. The woman's father would be insulted, and the entire tribe might decide to teach him some manners. If you ever fall for an Indian woman, make sure you court her properly.''

Nate laughed at the idea. "That will never happen.''

Now it was Shakespeare's turn to say nothing.

"Tell me more,'' Nate urged after a minute.

"Well, I can give you some pointers on Indian women in general. I've seen some real beauties in my time. Some trappers believe the Flathead women are the prettiest in general. Others think the Nez Perce women are the most beautiful. And I know quite a few who will swear by the Mandan women.''

"What about Cheyenne women?''

"Oh, they're right pretty in their own way. But everyone regards them most for their chastity. Unmarried Cheyenne women wear a leather chastity belt.''

Nate's mouth dropped, and he took several seconds to recover from the surprise. "They do?''

"Yep. The Cheyenne are firm believers in no sex before marriage. If a girl makes a mistake and lets herself be fondled beforehand, she earns a reputation for being immoral. And no Cheyenne girl wants that," Shakespeare related.

"But a chastity belt? They went out with the Middle Ages."

"I'd wager there are quite a number of white women back in the States who would have liked to be wearing a chastity belt at one time or another."

Nate shook his head in amazement. Would the wonders never cease? Who would have thought that Indian women would wear chastity belts? Yet, at the same time, they allowed themselves to be bought like an item of merchandise in a trading post. What a land of incredible contradictions!

"I was married to a Flathead woman about twenty years ago," Shakespeare mentioned. "And I always thought she was the loveliest creature ever put on this planet."

"What happened to her? Did you divorce her?"

"The damn Blackfeet killed her."

"Oh. I'm sorry to hear that," Nate said.

Shakespeare shrugged. "It was a long time ago. Of course, I've never forgiven the Blackfeet, and exterminate the savages every chance I get." He paused. "And about divorce. The Indians have a different attitude about it than the whites do."

"Do they allow divorce?"

"Sure do. In fact, it's a lot easier for an Indian to divorce than it is for those upright folks back in the States. If an Indian man wants a divorce, he goes through a ceremony and publicly announces he doesn't want her any more. All the woman has to do to be divorced is move back into her parents' lodge."

"An Indian woman can leave her husband?"

"If she wants. Few do." Shakespeare scratched his beard. "Even fewer fool around with other men."

"They must have high morals," Nate remarked.

"That, and the fact that any wife caught in the arms of another warrior has her nose cut off."

"Isn't that a bit extreme?"

"Not to the Indian way of thinking. You see, Indians put a lot of stock in public opinion. Most of them are scared to death at the notion of acquiring a bad reputation. Every warrior and maiden knows that if they get too far out of line, if they break the rules of the tribe, they could well have to walk about in shame for the rest of their lives."

"Every tribe is the same way?"

"The rules vary from tribe to tribe, and some are more severe than others. The Utes, for instance, don't cut off the nose of a woman found guilty of adultery."

"Now they sound civilized."

"Sometimes they whip her."

Nate began to suspect that Shakespeare was deliberately disclosing customs certain to shock him. "You make Indians out to be rather cruel," he commented to test his theory.

"Do I? That's certainly not my intention. Some of their practices are harsh by our standards, but Indians are not cruel by nature. In fact, I admire them highly. If I didn't, I wouldn't have spent the better part of my life living among them." He gazed at the ridge to their right. "For instance, Indians rarely spank their children."

Memories of all the beatings he had received as a youngster flashed through Nate's mind. "How do they discipline their children then?"

"By always instructing them in the right way to do things. Where a white parent might slap a child's face for not doing chores or whatever, an Indian parent will sit the child down and explain about the importance of always doing one's work and being honest and diligent. They're always loooking at the positive side of things."

"There must be some instances where they punish their children," Nate said.

"When the kids cry they're punished."

"Why? Aren't they allowed to cry?" Nate queried, half in jest.

"No."

"What harm can crying do?"

"Crying can get the whole tribe killed. Out here sounds can travel a long ways. An enemy war party could hear a child crying from far off and know where to find the camp. So Indian mothers are real strict about crying. They teach their babies not to cry at an early age."

Nate envisioned such a task as being impossible. "How can they stop a baby from crying? Crying is as natural as eating and sleeping."

"It's easy. Whenever a baby starts bawling, and if there's no apparent reason for it, the mother takes the baby away from the camp and hangs the cradleboard in a bush or on a tree. She leaves the baby there until the crying stops."

Nate thought of the grizzly he'd encountered. "That's heartless. What happens if a wild animal stumbles on the baby?"

"Rarely happens. Besides, most babies stop crying after two or three times out in the brush."

"I'd never do that to my child," Nate asserted.

Shakespeare abruptly reined up. "We sure are having a pitiful run of luck this trip."

"What do you mean?"

The frontiersman pointed at the ridge to the east. "Blackfeet."

Chapter Five

Nate twisted in his saddle and scanned the ridge, immediately spotting a large group of Indians who were riding over the crest, heading eastward. "They're going in the opposite direction," he declared in relief. "I don't think they saw us."

"Neither do I," Shakespeare agreed. "Keep your fingers crossed that none of those savages look back."

Nate watched the Blackfeet with bated breath, hoping there wouldn't be a repeat of their experience with the Utes. He was elated when the last warrior disappeared on the far side. "They're gone, and good riddance!"

"My sentiments exactly," Shakespeare said. "Although I could use a few more Blackfeet scalps to add to my collection." He chuckled and rode onward.

Pleased at their narrow escape from a potentially deadly encounter, Nate grinned as he followed his companion. He found himself speculating on why so many white men enjoyed the mountaineering life when there were so many varied and lethal dangers associated with such a hazardous existence. Was unbridled freedom that valuable? He'd enjoyed just a fleeting taste of wilderness life, and he had to admit he found the life appealing, infinitely more so than the drab routine of a bookkeeper in New York City. He stared at a golden eagle off to the west and marveled that he had once sought to have a career as a successful accountant.

They traveled for five hundred yards, and were angling into dense timber when a succession of gunshots arose to the east, from the other side of the ridge.

Shakespeare reined up and cocked his head. "Damn. Those Blackfeet must be after someone."

"Buffalo or elk maybe," Nate suggested. A second later he detected the faint sound of war whoops and realized he was wrong.

"Those Blackfeet aren't after game," Shakespeare said, turning his horse.

"What are you planning to do?"

"Go have a look-see."

Nate began to protest, but Shakespeare's next words caused him to hold his tongue.

"Those vermin could be attacking trappers en route to the rendezvous. Let's go."

"I'll be right behind you," Nate vowed, and let the older man lead the way. If white men were being attacked, then he had a duty to try and help them. He kept the mare close to the white horse as they galloped toward the ridge, the pack animal trailing behind them, amazed at his friend's horsemanship.

Shakespeare could ride as proficiently as an Indian, and his nimble mount took every obstacle in stride. He sped up the west slope of the ridge, using a narrow game trail, the same trail the Blackfeet had taken. Ten yards from the top he slowed his horse to a walk and cautiously approached the crest.

Nate nervously surveyed the rim, the Hawken in his right hand. What if the Blackfeet had posted a lookout?

The pressure of his pistols against his midriff was mildly reassuring. If worse came to worst, the Blackfeet would know they'd been in a fight. He saw Shakespeare stop and slip to the ground, and he did likewise.

The mountain man, keeping low, stepped to the rim.

Nate came up on Shakespeare's right and gazed at the scene below.

A beautiful valley about six miles long and three miles wide ran from the southeast to the northwest. Although trees were thick on the slopes of the surrounding mountains, in the valley there were few. The ground was covered with lush grass and herbage. Approximately a quarter of a mile from the west ridge was an Indian encampment consisting of 15 lodges, and the inhabitants of the village were now industriously engaged in defending themselves from the onslaught of 19 screeching Blackfeet.

Even as Nate watched, one of the defenders loosed an arrow and struck a Blackfoot warrior in the chest, toppling the attacker to the turf. But in the next few seconds he realized the defenders were hopelessly outnumbered. There only appeared to be three or four men in the whole village; the rest were women and children who were bravely assisting the few defending warriors as best they could.

"Damn!" Shakespeare exclaimed angrily. "I know them. You can stay here if you want." He wheeled and sprinted to his horse.

"I'm not staying put," Nate said, running to the mare. "Where you go, I go."

Shakespeare chuckled as he swung into the saddle. "If you make that your life's ambition, you might not live to see your hair turn gray."

"Are those Indians in the village friends of yours?" Nate asked as he climbed on his animal.

"Yep. They're Shoshones." Shakespeare urged his

mount upward. "Stay close and make every shot count."

Nate took a firm hold on his rifle and rode forward, feeling an equal mixture of excitement and trepidation. He resolved to give a good account of himself and not let Shakespeare down.

"Yell your lungs out once we hit the bottom," the frontiesman directed as he went over the crest.

"Why?"

"The more noise we create, the more we'll confuse those Blackfeet. They may get the notion that there's more of us than there are."

"But they'll see there's just the two of us."

"What they see doesn't matter. It's what we can make them *think* that counts. And they're bound to figure two white men wouldn't be crazy enough to attack them alone. They may jump to the conclusion there's more of us."

"Sounds awful risky," Nate noted, shifting his weight to compensate for the sharp slant of the slope.

"Not really. We'll be taking them by surprise. Out here, when a person is taken unawares, the best policy is to make tracks and count the enemy later. You live longer that way."

Nate glanced at the village. Several Blackfeet were already down, and one of the Shoshone warriors was on the ground, impaled by a lance. Two of the Shoshone women were also dead. The Blackfeet galloped around and through the encampment, firing their rifles and bows, but their elusive adversaries were difficult to hit. The Shoshones darted from lodge to lodge, dodging and weaving, always on the move.

Shakespeare broke his white horse into a gallop 15 yards from the base of the ridge and hit the valley floor in full stride. He uttered a piercing shriek that would have done justice to any Indian on the continent, and waved his rifle in the air.

Feeling as if his heart was in his throat, Nate followed suit, his left hand holding the lead to the pack animal. He glued his eyes to the battle, expecting the Blackfeet to spot them at any moment.

Embroiled in their intense conflict, none of the Indians were paying the slightest attention to the plain around the village.

Nate smiled grimly. This was perfect. The Blackfeet were too occupied to notice. If only the fight would continue for another minute.

A cluster of Shoshone women and children suddenly broke from the encampment, racing to the south, making toward the gully 40 yards distant. In the lead, urging on the others, was a young woman with flowing black hair down to her hips.

Five of the Blackfeet turned from the village, pursuing the women and children.

Nate released the pack horse and swerved to the right, forgetting all about staying close to Shakespeare in his concern for the Shoshones. He angled to intercept the Blackfeet, knowing full well he wouldn't arrive in time.

The young woman abruptly halted, motioned for the others to continue without her, and stooped to grab a rock. She faced the onrushing Blackfeet, her posture radiating defiance, and raised the rock overhead.

Admiration welled within Nate. What could she hope to accomplish wielding such a puny weapon other than to temporarily delay the warriors long enough for the rest of the women and the children to reach the gully? Bravery and pride were reflected in her carriage. His heart went out to her and he whipped the Hawken to his right shoulder.

The foremost Blackfoot, a husky warrior armed with a bow, approached the woman at an almost leisurely pace, smirking as he trained an arrow on her.

Would the warrior really fire? Nate wondered. Did Indian men slay the maidens in other tribes or merely take them captive? He couldn't afford to risk the woman's life on the chance the warrior might be bluffing, so he attempted to get a bead on the Blackfoot. The rocking motion of the mare made the task extremely difficult and he held off firing, covering another 30 yards in the process.

Laughing, the warrior lowered the bow.

The young woman shouted a word and hurled the rock.

Nate saw the Blackfoot rein sharply to the right, and the projectile missed. Clearly furious, the Shoshone woman scanned the grass near her feet for another stone.

Moving methodically, the warrior made a show of sighting another arrow on her breast.

It's now or never! Nate told himself. He fixed the front of the barrel on the Blackfoot, held his breath, and squeezed the trigger. Smoke and lead belched from the end of the Hawken.

One hundred and twenty yards distant, the warrior's mount unexpectedly buckled and pitched the Blackfoot onto the grass.

What a blockhead! Nate lowered the rifle and frowned. He'd missed the Indian and hit the horse! Now he'd wasted the shot, and he wasn't fast enough nor skilled enough to reload while riding at a full gallop before he reached the Blackfeet.

The warrior on the ground had risen to his knees and was recovering his bow. The other four had turned their animals at the retort of the Hawken and were gawking in frank astonishment.

Nate voiced a war whoop of his own, clutched the rifle and the reins in his left hand, and drew one of his pistols. He observed the Blackfeet glance to the north, where Shakespeare was bearing down on the village, and then look at him. The next few moments were crucial. Would the Blackfeet cut out or stay and fight?

One of the warriors hefted a war club and charged.

So much for Shakespeare's bright idea! Nate swung the mare to meet the Blackfoot head-on and made straight for him. Pistols were designed for short-range use, and unless he wanted to hazard wasting another ball, he had to get as close as practical to his opponent.

Whooping and swinging the club, the Blackfoot rapidly advanced.

The pounding of the mare's hooves drummed in Nate's ears as he closed. He kept the pistol next to his waist, screened by the animal's neck, his thumb on the hammer, his finger on the trigger. There was no sense in advertising how he intended to dispatch his adversary.

Two other warriors started toward him.

Nate focused on the first warrior to the exclusion of all else, acutely conscious of the shrinking yardage between them, anxious to fire but restraining the impulse until the proper moment. In the back of his mind he wondered if Shakespeare was faring all right. He couldn't venture a glance at the village to find out.

The Blackfoot vented his war cry once more and rose slightly on his mount, holding the club steady, ready to launch a downward stroke. Like most Indian weapons, the club had been embellished to suit the personal tastes of its owner. A sharp metal spoke projected from the blunt, rounded head, and the wooden handle was covered with elaborately decorated buckskin stitched together with sinew.

All of Nate's self-control barely sufficed to prevent him from shooting prematurely. At a distance of 20 yards the urge caused his fingers to twitch. At 15 yards, when he could clearly see the warrior's blazing eyes and flaring nostrils, he almost lifted the pistol from concealment. At ten yards he tensed, and at eight he swept his right arm up, extended the pistol, and fired.

The ball caught the Blackfoot at the base of his throat and propelled him over the rear of his animal to fall onto the hard earth with a thud. The war club went flying.

Nate looked down at his foe and saw the warrior thrashing violently, and then he had to stare straight ahead at the pair of Blackfeet converging on him. The one on the left reined up, but the warrior on the right came on strong.

This second warrior was armed with a fusee. Such rifles were smooth-bored flintlocks the Indians received in trade with the Hudson's Bay Company. The fusee the Blackfoot held had been shortened, as were many of the trade guns, to make the weapon easier to use while on horseback.

Nate remembered Shakespeare telling him that fusees were cheap, inferior weapons and no match for the rifles of the trappers and mountaineers. In fact, many Indians held the fusees in disdain and preferred to employ the traditional bow. At close range, though, a fuseee could be every bit as deadly as a Hawken even if it did lack the Hawken's accuracy and superb craftsmanship.

Gunshots were still sounding from the village.

Somewhere a woman screamed.

Alarmed, Nate looked at the young maiden with the flowing hair, relieved to see she wasn't being attacked. The Shoshone woman was simply standing there, watching him, perhaps astounded he had interjected himself into the battle or hoping he would emerge victorious. Her left hand was pressed to her neck. He spotted the warrior he had unhorsed standing a few dozen yards to the north, observing the progress of the fight.

The fight!

Startled by his lapse, Nate glanced at the charging Blackfoot who was now only 30 yards away. He quickly slid the empty pistol under his belt and drew the second one.

Both were smoothbore single-shot .55 caliber flintlocks, a matched set selected for him by his Uncle Zeke in St. Louis. They were powerful, but he had to get close to use them.

Apparently the Blackfoot had no intention of letting him come within range, because the warrior suddenly raised the fusee to his shoulder.

Chapter Six

Nate knew the Blackfoot would fire in the next few seconds. His pistol was no match for even the unreliable fusee at such a distance. He had to do something, and do it fast, or be shot.

But what?

What could he possibly do?

. He saw the warrior smile and expected to hear the fusee crack, and at that instant a flash of inspiration galvanized him into prompt action. He recalled the time he and Zeke had fought a party of marauding Kiowas, remembering the technique the Kiowa warriors had used to minimize the targets they'd presented. At the time he'd been taking a bead on one of them, and he'd been amazed to see the warrior slide onto the side of the galloping horse, using just a heel and a hooked arm to stay on board.

Could he do the same thing?

There was no time to debate the issue. He swung to the right, flattening against the mare, his left arm looped over the saddle, grasping the Hawken in his left hand. For added support he braced his left leg on the animal's broad back. The swaying motion threatened to dislodge him, but he held on for dear life.

He'd done it!

The Blackfoot couldn't see him, couldn't get a clear shot.

Nate gripped the pistol tightly, elated. Then a thought occurred to him and his exhilaration evaporated.

Yes, the Blackfoot couldn't see him.

But he couldn't see the warrior either.

Just great!

How was he supposed to defend himself? What if the Blackfoot changed direction? What if—and the idea brought goose bumps to his flesh—what if the warrior shot the mare instead? He eased forward as far as he could and peered under the mare's neck.

The Blackfoot was only 15 yards off. He'd slowed and straightened, striving to see over the side of the mare, the fusee flush with his shoulder.

Nate observed the warrior sight down the gun, and he realized the Blackfoot was going to shoot him in the arm or the leg to bring him down. He swiftly extended his arm, angled the pistol under the mare's neck, and fired.

A strident howl attended the blast as the ball hit the warrior in the left cheek and slammed the man from his mount.

Pulling himself up, Nate sat erect and glanced over his left shoulder. The Indian lay motionless on the ground. Two down and three to go, and that didn't include the Blackfeet attacking the village. To complicate matters, all three of his firearms were now empty.

Another warrior whooped and came on at a full charge.

Nate tucked the second pistol under his belt and slipped his butcher knife from its sheath. The knife was all he had left.

The third Blackfoot held a lance.

Nate recollected the tales Shakespeare and Zeke had

told him about the uncanny accuracy Indians could achieve with their slim spearlike weapons. They were trained in its use from boyhood, and a full-grown warrior could cast a lance 20 to 25 yards and consistently hit a target the size of a man's head, even when riding at full speed. He didn't stand a prayer armed with just a knife.

The warrior waved his lance and voiced a defiant challenge.

Nate urged the mare to go faster. He couldn't hope to outrun the Blackfoot. And the slower he went, the better target he would make. So his best bet seemed to be to gallop at the warrior and try to dodge the lance. Perhaps he could deflect the tip with his rifle. With that in mind he replaced the knife in its sheath and elevated the Hawken.

Wait a minute.

He knew the Hawken wasn't loaded, but the Blackfoot didn't. What would happen if he sighted on the warrior, if he pretended he was going to fire? There was only one way to find out. He pressed the stock to his shoulder and aimed at his enemy.

Executing an abupt turn, the Blackfoot lowered his lance and raced away to the south.

The ploy had worked!

Nate beamed and let the Hawken drop, overjoyed, congratulating himself on his cleverness. He saw the other Blackfeet hasten southward, including the warrior whose horse he'd accidentally killed, and his forehead creased in perplexity.

Why were they *all* running away?

He slowed, puzzled, and gazed at the maiden. She was beaming happily and staring past him, to the northwest. Was Shakespeare coming to his rescue? He looked over his left shoulder and tensed.

More Indians were rushing toward the village, 12 warriors bearing from the northwest, and in the lead rode a strapping warrior who wore only a breechcloth and carried a bow with a shaft at the ready. He led the band directly at the few Blackfeet still lingering in the vicinity of the lodges.

Nate reined up and swung the mare to view the conflict. He realized the dozen newcomers must be Shoshone warriors, returned to defend their families.

The majority of the Blackfeet had spied the Shoshones and fled, but three of the former were riding among the lodges, firing and hollering, oblivious to the fact the tide of battle had turned. They discovered their error seconds later.

Like a storm-tossed wave pounding the rocky shore of the Atlantic Ocean, the Shoshones fanned out and swept into their village. The tall leader drew his bowstring all the way back, sighting on a Blackfoot who was about to bash his war club against a boy's head, and let the arrow fly.

The shaft caught the Blackfoot between his shoulder blades, and the triangular tip and six inches of shaft burst out the center of his chest. He arched his back when he was struck, his mouth forming an oval, his eyes wide, then silently toppled to the ground.

In moments the other Shoshones dispatched the remaining Blackfeet. In one instance the Blackfoot was surrounded by seven Shoshones and brutally clubbed to death.

Absorbed in watching the battle, Nate nearly jumped out of the saddle when a hand fell on his right leg. He glanced down to find the young woman with the long hair.

She smiled up at him, her brown eyes studying him intently. Her dark tresses framed a face of uncommon beauty and accented her prominent cheekbones. A beaded buckskin dress covered her trim figure and moccasins adorned her feet.

"Hello," Nate said.

The woman spoke a sentence in the Shoshone tongue and regarded him inquisitively, apparently anticipating a reply.

Frustrated by his failure to understand, and wanting very much to communicate with her, Nate recalled the many lessons Zeke and Shakespeare had given him in Indian sign language, the universal means of exchanging information used by practically every tribe in the West. He extended the thumb and index finger on his right hand, curled the other fingers, then held the hand near his left breast. Next he moved his hand out and slightly up, turning his wrist as he did so, his palm becoming vertical. He was careful to have his thumb pointing to the front and the index finger pointing to the left. Keenly aware of her eyes on his hand, and hoping he was doing the sign language properly, he finished the response by opening his hand and sweeping it to the right and back again. There. If his memory had served him in good stead, he'd just told her that he didn't understand her language.

But what if he'd made a mistake?

What if he'd just stated that she looked like a fat buffalo cow?

The woman nodded, then pointed at the nearest Blackfoot he had shot. She extended both of her slender hands and held them flat, palms down. Sweeping them upward, she angled them down toward Nate.

She was saying thank you! Incredibly relieved, Nate grinned and made the proper signs to ask her name.

"Winona," she revealed.

"Nate," he said, tapping his chest. "Nate King."

"Nate King," Winona repeated slowly, speaking each word crisply, duplicating his pronunciation with remarkable facility. "Nate King. Nate King."

Her melodic voice thrilled Nate to his core. He tried

to think of something else he could say, feeling oddly self-conscious about his inexperience and ignorance.

Winona's hands began making signs at a rapid clip.

Struggling to keep up, Nate leaned down to catch every movement. Some of the signs she used were foreign to him. He gathered that she was telling him his medicine must be very great to have slain so many Blackfeet, but he couldn't be certain. She stopped and looked at him as if awaiting a reply, and at that awkward moment he heard the drumming of hooves and straightened to face the village.

Shakespeare, the tall Shoshone, and five other warriors were riding toward them.

Nate became aware of the tall Shoshone's gaze focused on himself, and he wondered why he should be the object of such an intense scrutiny. He realized he'd neglected to reload and chided himself for being a dunderhead.

"Well, well, well," Shakespeare said as he drew to a stop. He gazed at the dead Blackfeet. "You've been a mite busy, I see."

"And what about you?"

"I took care of three of the rascals, and good riddance," Shakespeare said. "Strike! Down with them! Cut the villains' throats! Ah! Whoreson caterpillars! Bacon-fed knaves! They hate us, youth. Down with them! Fleece them!" He gestered wildly as he spoke.

"What?" Nate asked, wondering if the frontiersman was putting on an act.

"William S."

"Oh."

The strapping Shoshone abruptly addressed Winona, and she answered with a torrent of words, gesturing repeatedly at the slain Blackfeet and at Nate. After a minute the tall warrior looked solemnly at Shakepeare and spoke a few words.

"What did they say?" Nate queried.

Shakespeare chuckled. "You never cease to amaze me."

"I do?"

"Yep." The frontiersman indicated the tall Shoshone. "This here is Black Kettle, a prominent man in the Shoshone nation. Winona there is his daughter. She just gave him a blow-by-blow description of your fight. Says you saved her life and the lives of the women and children with her." He snickered. "She also says you are the bravest fighter who ever lived and the second greatest man in existence, her father being the greatest, of course."

Nate didn't know what to say.

"Yes, sir," Shakespeare commented. "You've made quite a mark."

"I was just trying to stay alive."

Black Kettle glanced at the mountain man and voiced an extended discourse.

"He says he is in your debt," Shakespeare translated after the Shoshone finished. "He says he owes you for the life of his precious daughter and his beloved people."

"I did what I had to," Nate said. "He doesn't owe me a thing."

"Don't expect me to tell him that."

"Why not?"

"Remember what I told you about being mighty careful not to insult an Indian? If he wants to be in your debt, let him. Having an Indian be in your debt is a lot better than having an Indian try to scalp you," Shakespeare observed.

"What do I do? What do I tell him?"

"I'll handle the conversation," Shakespeare declared. "He wants to know your name. Now let me see." His forehead furrowed and he scratched his head. "What was that name the Cheyennes gave you?"

"You can quote Shakespeare but you can't remember

a simple thing like that?''

"Oh. Now I remember. Grizzly Killer.'' Shakespeare turned to Black Kettle and went on at length in the Shoshone tongue.   •

Again Nate was the object of the tall warrior's undivided attention. To cover his embarrassment, Nate gazed at the village and sw a party of six Shoshones ride off in pursuit of the fleeing Blackfeet. The women and children were returning to their lodges. He glanced down at Winona and gave her his friendliest smile.

Black Kettle replied to Shakespeare, who then interpreted.

"If it will make you feel any better, he says he's in debt to both of us. His family is on their way to the rendezvous and he's invited us to tag along. How does the notion strike you?''

"Just fine.''

"I figured it might.''

"I'll have the opportunity to learn some of their language.''

"And I admire a man who's never too old to learn,'' Shakespeare said with a twinkle in his eyes.

"Would you accept his invitation and thank him for his kindness?''

"Now why didn't I think of that?'' Shakespeare spoke to Black Kettle for half a minute, listened to the Shoshone's response, and stared at his companion. "He's delighted. He plans to have us for supper.''

"Tell him not to bother going to so much trouble.''

"There you go again.''

"What do you mean?'' Nate queried, and insight dawned. "Oh, Sorry. It's just force of habit.''

"I know, but it's a habit you'd better break and fast. When you live with the Indians, you live by Indian rules.''

"There's so much to know.''

"Let me give you some sound advice," Shakespeare offered. "When in doubt, keep your mouth shut and your ears open. You'll live longer that way."

"I'll do my best," Nate vowed.

"Oh. And one more thing."

"What?"

"How do you feel about getting married?"

Chapter Seven

"What's that supposed to mean?" Nate demanded.

Shakespeare grinned. "The young filly you saved has her sights set on you."

Nate looked down at Winona, who smiled sweetly at him, then at the frontiersman. "You're crazy."

"You are already Love's firm votary, and cannot soon revolt and change your mind."

"What?"

Shakespeare chuckled and quoted more of his favorite author. "But love, first learned in a lady's eyes, lives not alone immured in the brain. But, with the motion of all elements, courses as swift as thought in every power, and gives to every power a double power, above their functions andd offices."

"Sometimes I don't understand a word you say," Nate said testily. "Why can't you use English like everyone else?"

"Use English?" Shakespeare repeated, and erupted into a fit of laughter, rocking back and forth in the saddle, his eyes closed. "Use English!" he roared, and laughed harder.

The Shoshones stared at the mountain man as if he were a madman.

Annoyed, Nate occupied his time by reloading the Hawken. He wedged the rifle under his left leg, poured the amount of black powder he would need from the powder horn into the palm of his left hand, then fed the powder down the muzzle. Next he took a ball from his bullet pouch, wrapped the ball in a patch and used his thumb to start both down the barrel, and concluded by shoving the ball the rest of the way down with the ramrod. When he finished and glanced up he was surprised to find all of the Shoshones watching him. He smiled at them and gazed at Shakespeare, who was still smiling. ''Why are they all looking at me?''

''They don't own many guns. They're just curious.''

Black Kettle pointed at the Blackfeet Nate had slain and addressed the frontiersman.

''This should be interesting,'' Shakespeare said when the warrior was done.

''Does he want us to bury them?'' Nate guessed.

''No, nothing like that,'' Shakespeare replied. ''He'll have the bodies taken into the village, but first he figured you'd want to scalp the ones you killed.''

Nate inadvertently tensed. ''Scalp them?''

''Yep. What's wrong? You scalped that Kiowa warrior who killed your Uncle Zeke.''

''I told you I didn't know if I could ever take another,'' Nate reminded him.

''Don't be squeamish now. If you don't take the hair off those Blackfeet, the Shoshones will think you're less than a man.''

''Just because I don't want to slice someone's hair off?''

''You know how important scalps are to these people. Some tribes are downright fanatical about it. The Crows, for instance, consider a man who won't kill and scalp his enemies as a weakling and an insult to the tribe. He's not allowed to carry weapons or take part in any of the activities the men do. Instead he's made a slave of the women. He has to do anything the women tell him. Tote water. Chop wood. Dress hides. You name it. Believe me, Nate, any Crow warrior who falls into the womens' ranks can't wait to be given the chance to prove himself and regain his manhood."

"They're not going to make a slave of me."

"No, but they'll tell everybody they meet about the white man who wouldn't scalp an enemy he bested in fair combat, and you'll acquire a reputation worse than a polecat's."

Nate tried to keep his features inscrutable as he looked at Black Kettle. He was trapped by Indian custom. He didn't necessarily want to scalp the Blackfeet, but he'd learned enough about life in the wilderness to appreciate the critical importance of an unsullied reputation. "Tell Black Kettle I thank him. Yes, I would like to scalp the warriors I killed."

Shakespeare nodded slowly. "Figured you would." He spoke to Black Kettle.

Cradling the Hawken in his left arm, Nate wheeled the mare and rode to the closest Blackfoot, the one he had shot in the cheek. He dismounted, placed the Hawken on the ground, and drew his butcher knife.

The warrior lay on his back, his eyes wide and glazing.

Nate took a deep breath, knelt, and grasped the Blackfoot's hair in his left hand. He tilted the head and carefully inserted the tip of the knife at the hairline above the forehead. Blood trickled onto the blade and down over the warrior's eyes. Working swiftly, he pried the knife under the hair and neatly separated the scalp from the head. He studiously avoided staring at the grisly, crimson-splotched pate underneath, and instead grabbed his

Hawken, stood, and led the mare to the Blackfoot he had shot in the throat.

A pool of bright blood had collected about the warrior's head, forming a liquid halo, and more blood continued to seep from the hole. The Blackfoot's mouth was opened wide, and he seemed to have died when about to scream his vented terror to the impassive heavens.

This time Nate worked even faster, and in less than a minute he held both scalps in his left hand. He wiped the knife clean on the grass, replaced the weapon in its sheath, clutched the Hawken in his right hand and mounted the mare.

Shakespeare and the Shoshones were waiting for him.

"Smartly done," the mountain man observed as Nate rode up.

"I didn't realize I'd have an audience."'

"You've impressed Black Kettle. He just told me he thinks you have the makings of a mighty warrior."

"If he only knew."

"Don't sell yourself short, Nate. Stranger things have happened."

Black Kettle said a few words to Winona, then motioned with his right arm and headed for the village, trailed by the five warriors.

"What did he say to her?" Nate said.

Shakespeare laughed lightly. "He instructed her to remember she's a lady."

"Why in the world would he tell her that?"

A peculiar snort, much like the noise made by a young bull frolicking in a pasture with a bovine playmate, issued from the frontiersman. "I hope you won't mind me saying this, and please don't take offense, but you are downright pitiful."

"In what way?"

"In every way, my young friend." Shakespeare nodded

at the Shoshone village. "Let's go to Black Kettle's lodge.
His people will tend to the mess. One of his warriors is
fetching our pack horse."

Perplexed and feeling slightly hurt, Nate rode along
slowly with Shakespeare on his left and Winona walking
beside his mare on the right. "I'll expect a full explanation
later," he stated peevishly.

"Life will be your explanation."

"Sometimes you make no sense whatsoever."

"Never forget, Nate, that one man's ignorance is
another man's past."

Nate sighed. "I'll remember it, but I'll be damned if
I know what it means."

Winona interjected a string of remarks in Shoshone,
directing them at Shakespeare.

"Anything I should know?" Nate inquired when he
finished.

"She wants to know if you're married."

Nate almost dropped the scalps.

"I warned you. She's got the notion into her dainty head
that you're the rip-roaringest thing in pants, and if there's
one fact I've learned during my long and eventful life,
it's this: Women never give up once they've fixed their
sights on a man. Nine times out of ten they'll bag the man
they want, and the one exception can usually be blamed
on circumstances they can't control. I don't care if it's
a white woman or an Indian, a black or a Chinese, an
Egyptian or Helen of Troy, they get the man they want."
He chuckled and shook his head. "Of course, another fact
I've learned is that women are never satisfied once they
have their men. Remember this, Nate. There's no pleasing
a woman. Anyone who tries to tell you different has his
brains below his belt."

Nate smiled down at Winona, and there was no denying
the incipient affection in her lively eyes. "Somehow I had

the idea Indian woman were shy and retiring.''

''The shy ones are the worst. They lay the cleverest traps.''

''You seem to equate romance with hunting and going after game.''

''You've just hit the nail on the head. Romance is a hunt, and for a woman it's the grandest hunt of all. She throws her wits and her charms into the chase, and the lure she uses is practically irresistible.''

''I think you're exaggerating.''

''Time will tell.''

''You can let her know I'm not married,'' Nate said. ''And whatever else she wants to know.''

''As you wish, young squire.''

''Huh?''

''Remind me to find you a book on Shakespeare. You could use a little of William S.'s wisdom.''

''I could use a drink.''

They came to the edge of the village. Bodies lay scattered about, the corpses of men, women, and a few children. The Blackfeet had been relentlessly ruthless in their attack. With sorrow lining their features the Shoshones were going about the miserable business of attending to their dead.

''Shouldn't we help them?'' Nate inquired.

''They wouldn't want our help. This is a private matter to them.''

Winona unexpectedly dashed off to aid an elderly woman who had sustained a scalp wound and was shuffling around a nearby lodge.

''Why did the Blackfeet kill women and children? What honor could there be in slaying those who are defenseless?''

''Defenseless?'' Shakespeare repeated, and snorted. ''Where'd you ever get a notion like that? It's true the men do most of the warring, but the women and young'uns are far from defenseless. Both will defend their village when it's attacked. Indian boys can shoot a bow as soon as they're old enough to hold one, and Indian women are no slouches when they're riled. In some tribes women are even allowed to go on raids. The Utes let a woman go along if she wants.''

"They do?" Nate said in surprise.

"Yep. Remember that. You might find yourself on the business end of a lance held by a pretty woman some day. What would you do if it happens?"

"I'd do everything in my power not to harm the woman."

Shakespeare smiled. "You would, huh?"

"I don't know if I could help myself. I was raised to be a gentleman around ladies."

"Ladies are nothing but ordinary women with high airs and fancy clothes. And if you don't change that attitude of yours, you could end up as a *dead* gentleman."

"Have you ever killed a woman?"

Shakespeare glanced sharply at his companion: "There are some questions you should never ask a man, not even a friend."

"Sorry."

"Here we are," Shakespeare announced, and reined up in front of one of the lodges. "This is Black Kettle's teepee."

"His what?"

"Teepee. It's a Sioux word for lodge."

Nate studied the structure before them. The general shape reminded him of the haystacks he had seen on farms. A number of pine poles had been placed on end in the shape of a large circle, then secured together at the top. Dressed buffalo hides served as the outer covering; they had been sewn together and stretched over the pole framework. He estimated the height to be 25 or 30 feet and the diameter of the base to be 20 feet.

"We'll have to wait for Black Kettle before we can go in," Shakespeare mentioned. "In the meantime I'll fill you in on how to behave."

"What do you mean?"

"There are certain rules you need to know. Do you see that door there?" Shakespeare asked, and nodded at a closed flap.

"Yes."

"If the door is open you can enter a lodge without bothering about formality, but if the door is closed you can't go in until after you let those inside know you're there and get an invite. Understand?"

"Yes."

"Once you're in, go to the right and wait for the man of the lodge to ask you to sit down."

"Go to the right? Why can't I go to the left?"

Shakespeare sighed. "Because the women go to the left. Are you a woman?"

"No, of course not."

"Then go to the right. The head of the lodge will likely want you to sit on his left. On your way to the spot never pass between the fire and another person."

"Why not?"

"The Indians consider it rude and a bad sign."

"You're kidding?"

"Where's a war club when I need one?"

"What?"

"Just pay attention. Always walk behind people seated around a fire. If you're invited to eat, eat. And you'd damn well better eat every morsel. Don't leave a crumb or you'll insult your host."

Nate shook his head in amazement. "I had no idea."

"I'm not done yet. If the head of the lodge taps his pipe

on the ground or asks his woman to unroll his blanket, it's the signal to leave.''

"Do I leave on the right side?"

"No. You fly out the ventilation flap at the top," Shakespeare answered, and cackled. He slid to the ground and turned.

Nate climbed down, his mouth twisted in a wry smile. He heard a mournful wail, and pivoted to behold three Shoshone warriors bearing a fourth between them. Walking alongside was a woman with tears pouring from her eyes. Her hands were pressed to her cheeks and she sobbed pitiably.

"I'm glad you've gotten over your squeamishness," Shakespeare commented.

"Why's that?" Nate inquired.

"Because you're about to see some sights that can freeze your blood in your veins."

Chapter Eight

Shakespeare, as it turned out, had uttered the understatement of the century.

While some Shoshones tended to the wounded, others gathered the dead. Three slain Shoshone warriors, five women, and three young boys were laid out in a row near Black Kettle's lodge. Then the dead Blackfeet were collected, 11 in all, and arranged in a line ten yards to the south.

Nate observed the proceedings expectantly. He saw the wives of the three deceased warriors throw themselves on the bodies of their husbands, where the women lamented their fate to the heavens and sobbed profusely. The mothers and sisters of the young boys likewise displayed their anguish. But the men vented their sorrow differently.

Black Kettle and the other Shoshone warriors walked to their fallen foes, took out knives, and commenced to cutting out the hearts, livers, and other organs, all the while voicing piercing yells and howls.

Aghast at the atrocity he was witnessing, Nate leaned close to Shakespeare. "Why are they mutilating the

Blackfeet?''

"They're taking revenge for their own people who were killed.''

"But the Blackfeet are already dead.''

"Doesn't matter a lick to them.''

Nate recoiled in revulsion when the Shoshones began to cut the organs into bits and pieces and then tossed the chunks to the village dogs, which had materialized as if out of nowhere after the battle ended. He bowed his head, feeling a bitter bile rise in his mouth, and when he looked up again the horror had worsened.

The Shoshones were hacking off the heads of the Blackfeet.

"This is the part I like the best,'' Shakespeare commented.

Slicing methodically, the Shoshones severed every last Blackfoot head. They each grabbed a grisly trophy in each hand and began to dance and prance, triumphantly waving the heads, shouting in exultation. The women and the children watched happily, beaming in innocent delight.

"Dear God in heaven!'' Nate breathed.

Shakespeare heard and glanced at his companion. "The white man's God don't count for much west of the Mississippi. Most of the tribes believe in the Great Spirit or the Great Medicine. They're very religious in their way.''

Nate stared at the Shoshones gloating and cavorting in primitive abandon. "You call these people religious?''

"You've got to remember that one man's God is another man's devil.''

"Meaning what?''

"Don't judge Indians by our values.''

"They're savage by any standard.''

"So what if they are? Who's to say white men are any better than them just because the whites are supposedly civilized?''

Appalled, Nate looked at the frontiersman. ''Do you approve of this barbaric conduct?''

''I won't lie to you. Yes, I do.''

Nate took a half step backwards, his abhorrence transparent. ''*How can you?*''

''It's the call of the wild.''

''The what?''

''The call of the wild. The lure of the wilderness. A zest for life. Whatever you want to call the feeling that grows inside a man if he stays out here long enough. You label the Shoshones as barbaric for defeating their enemies in fair combat and then taking pride in their accomplishment. At least they're open about it. They're honestly in touch with their inner feelings,'' Shakespeare said. ''That's more than I can say for the white man. Our kind hide their feelings behind a wall of laws, or they deny their feelings rather than offend someone else. If two whites have a dispute, and if they're too cowardly to settle the issue with a duel, one might sue the other and let a court settle the affair. They never really face their enemy or their own emotions. If they lose, they act as if it doesn't matter when deep down they want to beat the other fellow to a pulp.''

Nate gazed at the Shoshones and said nothing.

''Out here a man enjoys true freedom, the freedom of the wilderness. And if there's one lesson the wilderness teaches every mother's son, it's this: If you bite off more than you can chew, you pay the price. Big bite, little bite, it doesn't matter. Those Blackfeet bit off more than they could chew, and now the Shoshones are doing what comes naturally.'' Shakespeare paused. ''Do you understand what I'm trying to tell you?''

''I think so.''

''Civilization cushions folks from their own mistakes, Nate. Someone in St. Louis or New York doesn't have to worry about going hungry if they miss a deer or an elk. They can walk down to the corner market and buy all the food they need. And they don't have to fret about dying of thirst if they get lost and can't find a spring or a stream. They can get a drink just about anywhere.''

Nate listened with half an ear, his gaze on the Shoshones as they scalped the heads of the Blackfeet.

"Civilization is the haven of bullies and the weak," Shakespeare went on. "A bully can get away with pushing folks around in a big city because he knows few of them will have the gumption to stand up to him. But any man who tries to impose on another out here is likely as not to be shot for his effort.''

The Shoshone warriors were now impaling the heads on lances and proudly swinging the lances in the air.

"And in the wilderness a man can't afford to be weak. It's true what they say about only the strong surviving, and sometimes even the strong ones don't make it. Look at what happened to your Uncle Zeke,'' Shakespeare mentioned.

Nate glanced at the mountain man. "Then why bother?"

"Beg pardon?"

"Why do so many white men come west of the Mississippi to live, to hunt and trap and mingle with the Indians, if life here is so hard and filled with danger? If one little mistake, like leaning down to get a drink from a spring and not checking the rocks for rattlesnakes, can get you killed, why bother staying? Is the freedom you keep talking about worth all the trouble?''

"That's a decision you'll have to make on your own. It's worth more than all the gold in Creation to me, but it might not be worth a cent to you.''

"I just don't know," Nate said slowly.

The Shoshone warriors carried the impaled heads to the southern edge of the camp. Once there, they proceeded to dash the heads to the ground repeatedly, smashing the faces to a pulp and splitting several of the Blackfeet craniums. Brains and gore spattered the earth.

"Why don't they just bury the bodies and be done with it?" Nate asked distastefully.

"Indians never bury the dead of their enemies. Why should they send a foe off in style into the Great Mystery? Besides, you've got to bear in mind that Indians don't view dead bodies the same way whites do."

"So I've noticed."

"Let me explain. It's possible for a warrior to count coup on a dead body—"

"What?" Nate interrupted in surprise. "I thought they counted coup by touching live foes or killing them."

"It's more complicated than that. Some tribes let up to four men count coup on the same enemy. The Crow and Arapahoe do. The Cheyenne, on the other hand, only allow three men to count coup. And the Assiniboin won't permit the counting of any coup unless the body has been touched, whether it's alive or dead."

Nate shook his head. "I'm confused," he admitted.

"Let me try to clear it up for you," Shakespeare offered in the manner of a schoolteacher. "Let's say two tribes are fighting, the Crow and the Blackfeet. One of the Crows strikes one of the Blackfeet with his war club, and the Crow gets to claim first coup, the highest honor, because he struck the Blackfoot while the man was still alive. Then let's say another Crow comes along while the Blackfoot is lying wounded and this second Crow actually kills the Blackfoot. This second Crow can claim second coup, a lesser honor. Follow me so far?"

"So far."

"All right. Then let's say yet a third Crow comes along, and he's the one who scalps the dead Blackfoot. The third Crow can claim third coup, an even lesser honor but still a coup. To round this up, a fourth Crow comes by and cuts the heart out of the Blackfoot. He has fourth coup, which isn't much, but a warrior will take every coup he gets."

"Why didn't the first Crow do the killing and the scalping and all the rest?" Nate questioned.

"You've been in a few scrapes now. You know how hectic a fight can be. Sometimes a warrior will wound an enemy but doesn't have the time to finish the job," Shakespeare said.

"The way you explain it all makes perfect sense," Nate stated. "But I still don't much like the notion of carving an enemy into pieces. That's the work of a butcher."

"War is butchery. Don't let anyone tell you different."

The Shoshone men reentered the village and joined the women and children around their fallen tribe members. The warriors went to their fallen companions and addressed the three dead Shoshone warriors in the most earnest terms.

"What are they doing?" Nate asked, thoroughly perplexed by the sight of grown men talking to lifeless corpses.

"They're letting their friends know that they took revenge on the Blackfeet."

"But their friends are dead."

"There you go again, thinking in white man's terms," Shakespeare admonished the younger man. "If the Indians view everything from eating to fighting differently than us, doesn't it stand to reason they'd view the dead differently too?"

Nate simply nodded.

"You've got to remember that most Indians believe in an afterlife. These Snakes believe that the souls of the dead watch over the living. Each warrior has his own guardian angel, as it were."

"Wait a minute. You just called them Snakes. I thought they were the Shoshones."

"Shoshone is their own word for their tribe. Most whites call them the Snakes, probably because they spend a lot of the year in the regions around the head branches of the Snake River, although they'll travel all the way over the Divide to the Plains for buffalo when they're in the need."

The sound of approaching horses drew the attention of everyone in the camp to the southeast, and moments later the six Shoshones who had raced in pursuit of the Blackfeet rode into view from a stand of trees.

"We might as well get comfortable," Shakespeare advised. "This will take a while." He sat down on the ground cross-legged and placed his rifle across his lap.

Nate remained standing, not wanting to miss a single moment of the spectacle. In his mind's eye he saw himself back in the comfort and safety of New York, relating to Adeline and his family the many harrowing experiences he'd survived while living in the wilderness. Being Easterners born and bred, they would undoubtedly be particularly interested in any and all Indian customs, and here was a firsthand opportunity to observe those practices often held in mystified dread by the whites.

The six warriors pounded into the village and promptly dismounted. One of them whooped while proudly displaying the body of a Blackfoot he'd ridden down and killed. He held the body erect with his left arm and hit it several times with his war club while reciting his coup.

Nate's eyes narrowed at the sight of the Blackfoot. He recognized the enemy warrior as the same one he'd unhorsed by accidentally shooting the man's animal. So indirectly he was responsible for that Blackfoot's death. Add another life to the tally! he thought bitterly. He was still troubled by shadowy notions of what would happen to his own soul after all the killing he had done. He'd never been excessively religious, but he'd attended church regularly in his younger years and he could quote the Ten Commandments by rote. Thou shalt not kill.

Couldn't get much clearer than that.

Nate looked down at his hands. Strange, though, how with all the death on his hands they were still the same hands and he was still basically the same person. Taking the lives of others hadn't resulted in any great, profound, or terrible insights of self-discovery. Slaying them hadn't altered him one bit as far as he could see. Although, deep down, he'd realized that taking the lives of the last two Blackfeet had been emotionally easier to do than taking the life of the first man he'd killed.

Was that the way it happened?

The idea troubled him. What if each killing became easier and easier? What was to stop him from shooting people for the sheer spiteful meanness of the deed? What separated a basically decent, honest peson like him from cold-blooded murderers? There must be some higher quality or capacity he possessed that served to distinguish him morally and spiritually from common, vile killers?

But what?

A sharp cry came from the Shoshones.

Nate glanced up, startled.

Apparently the Snakes did not intend to make the burial of their dead an elaborate ritual. Some of them had gone to the east side of the village and were busily engaged in digging graves. Others were collecting buffalo robes and other items. Those women connected by blood or marriage to the deceased were clinging to the corpses and wailing pitiably, seemingly striving to attest to the depth of their love by the volume of their cries.

"I heard one of them talking," Shakespeare mentioned loudly to be heard over the crying. "Ordinarily they'd wait a day to plant the bodies in the ground, but when Black Kettle and his hunting party were out earlier they found sign of a large number of Blackfeet in the area. That's why they came back when they did. They're fixing to leave first thing tomorrow morning.''

"How many Blackfeet?" Nate asked absently.

"About fifty."

"Fifty?" Nate repeated, glancing at the mountain man. "Why would there be so many Blackfeet in this area now of all times? They must know that every white man in the country and many of the friendly tribes are gathering for the annual rendezvous?"

"That's *why* the Blackfeet are here," Shakespeare stressed. "They roam around the countryside like vultures, preying on any small groups of whites or Indians they find. They know about the rendezvous and they figure this is a golden opportunity to settle old scores."

Nate envisioned hordes of savage Blackfeet descending upon helpless travelers, slaughtering the innocents in droves. "Can't anything be done about them?"

Shakespeare chuckled. "Well, a lot of folks, whites and Indians, are doing a right smart job of exterminating the varmints every chance they get."

"I'm serious."

"What would you do then?"

"Why, I'd raise an army and wipe them out or drive them all the way into Canada if need be."

"There you go again. You really are a bloodthirsty cub. Where do you think you're going to get this army of yours? From the other Indian tribes? How do you think the Blackfeet got to be the top dogs in the northern Rockies and on the high plains? They whipped every other tribe, that's how. The Blackfeet have beaten the Nez Perce, the Flatheads, the Crow, and the Shoshones time and time again. They've taken the choicest land for themselves and driven the others into the high valleys. There isn't a tribe north of the Yellowstone River that would stand a snowball's chance in Hades of defeating the Blackfeet.''

"Then what about the whites? Why do they tolerate the situation?''

"Probably because there aren't more than four or five hundred white men scattered about the entire West from the Mississippi to the Pacific Ocean and from Canada to Santa Fe, not counting the state of Missouri.''

"So how many Blackfeet are there?''

"I don't know exactly. Thousands, at least. I'd guess eight or ten thousand.''

"I didn't realize," Nate said blankly.

Shakespeare glanced at the Shoshones, who were busily attending to their burial preparations, and faced his friend. "Let me tell you a story. About five years ago someone had the exact same notion you did about raising an army, only they were going after the Rickarees, not the Blackfeet.''

"Someone really raised an army?''

"Let me finish, will you? Early in '23 a gent by the name of Ashley led about seventy men out of St. Louis on his way into trapping country. He got as far as the Rickaree villages way up on the Missouri River. There his men were attacked by six hundred warriors, and he lost twelve before he could cut out and head back downstream. He sent a letter to good old Colonel Henry Leavenworth, old blood and guts himself,'' Shakespeare related. "Well, the colonel got together about two hundred white men, rounded up a pair of cannons and some swivel guns, and marched north to pit his army against the Rickarees and teach those heathens a lesson.'' Here the frontiersman stopped and laughed.

"What's so funny?''

"Never mind. Now where was I? Oh, yes. Along the

way the colonel was joined by pretty near seven hundred Sioux. The Sioux, you see, can't abide the Rickarees, so they were right eager to help give their enemies a licking. Colonel Leavenworth named his army the Missouri Legion, and before the Legion finally showed up outside the Rickaree villages, he'd collected more whites and stray Indians until he had well over a thousand fighting men under his command.''

"The Rickarees must have been destroyed," Nate predicted.

Again Shakespeare laughed. "You'd think so, wouldn't you? Well, the Rickarees couldn't help but notice an army that size approaching their village, so they did the only sensible thing they could do.''

"They fought to the last warrior.''

"No. They ran.''

"The cowards!" Nate opined.

"Cowardice is like bravery, Nate. Sometimes it's relative to the occasion. What good would it have done those Rickarees to be wiped out to the last man, or to have their wives and children slaughtered by the Sioux?''

Nate didn't respond. The answer was obvious.

"So the Rickarees retreated under the cover of darkness and left their village unattended.''

"And Colonel Leavenworth burned the villages and returned without a decisive victory," Nate concluded, deducing the rest of the tale. Or so he thought.

"Wrong. Colonel Leavenworth laid siege to the empty villages. For days his Legion tippy-toed around the villages, just out of rifle and bow range, while he bombarded them with cannon rounds to convince them he was deadly serious.''

"You're joking me.''

Shakespeare snorted. "The joke was on Colonel Leavenworth and the Missouri Legion. They made complete and utter fools of themselves. The white man became the laughingstock of the Rickarees and their allies, and the whites lost prestige in the eyes of every other tribe who heard the report, even the friendly tribes. The upper Missouri has been pretty much closed to white trappers ever since because the Rickarees are no longer afraid of us.''

"But the idea for an army is still sound. It would have worked if Leavenworth had defeated the Rickarees.''

"Even if he had, he certainly didn't have enough men to conquer the Blackfeet. No, you might as well get used to the notion that the Blackfeet will be around for years to come. If you should decide to stay out here, they'll be your worst enemies.''

Nate was about to make a comment when a piercing wail drew his attention to the Shoshone women gathered around the fallen warriors.

One of them had just hacked off the tip of her finger.

Chapter Nine

"Dear Lord!" Nate exclaimed.

Someone had brought a large, flat rock and placed it on the ground near the three deceased Shoshone warriors. Five women were gathered around the rock, and one of them, the woman who had just sliced off the end of her left forefinger at the first joint, was on her knees, a bloody hunting knife clutched in her right hand.

"Why?" Nate blurted.

The woman lowered the knife onto the rock, then used the stump of her left forefinger to smear streaks of blood on her cheeks. The entire time her face radiated supreme pride in her accomplishment. She slowly stood and stepped aside so another woman could kneel.

"They're the wives of the dead men," Shakespeare explained reverently. "They're mourning the loss of their husbands and showing their devotion."

Stunned by the sight, and not knowing what else to say, Nate commented on the obvious. "But there are five women."

"Many tribes believe in plural marriages. What with all the warfare and the dangers entailed in just going hunting, there's a regular shortage of men.''

The second woman now applied the knife to the tip of one of her fingers and cut the digit off without betraying the slightest qualm. It was another of the attending women who let out a wail as if in commiseration. One by one the five women each severed part of a finger and painted their faces with their own blood.

"They keep that blood on until it wears off," Shakespeare remarked.

Next the Shoshones wrapped the dead in buffalo robes and carried the bodies to the freshly dug graves. First the three warriors were lowered into the earth, then the five women and the boys.

Nate expected the graves to be promptly filled, but he was mistaken.

The Shoshones began depositing items in the holes: weapons in the case of the men, bows and arrows and war clubs—and one man even had a clipped horse's tail added to the pile; blankets, trinkets, and porcupine-tail hairbrushes were laid to rest with the women; and the boys were the recipients of weapons or other effects.

"What are they doing?" Nate inquired.

"When Indians are buried, their favorite personal possessions and talismans get buried with them."

"Why?"

"They believe that the dead wake up in the next world with whatever is buried with the departed. Did you see that horse's tail they put in one of the graves?"

"Yes."

"They hold that each of those hairs will change into a sturdy steed in the spirit land."

Nate regarded the Shoshones critically. "I'll never understand the Indian way of life if I live to be a hundred."

A wry smile creased the frontiersman's lips. "Therefore, good Nate, be prepared to hear this. Since you cannot see yourself so well as by reflection, I your glass will modestly discover to yourself that of yourself which you yet know not of." He paused. "With apologies to Brutus."

"What?"

"I'll talk to you again in a year or so."

Mystified by the mountain man's words, Nate shook his head and observed the conclusion of the burial ceremony.

A number of Shoshones began beating drums and sticks while several warriors attended to filling in the graves. The rest of the tribe began a short procession, with the tribal members singing, yelling, and dancing in a slow, shuffling step. They made three circuits of the graves, then halted and gave voice to a melodic chant.

"We're lucky in a way," Shakespeare mentioned.

"How so?"

"These affairs can drag on for days. If Black Kettle wasn't concerned about the Blackfeet, we'd miss even more of the rendezvous than we already will."

"Can't we just leave when we feel so inclined?"

"We could, if you don't care about insulting Black Kettle. I'll wait this out. He'll probably be leaving tomorrow morning and we can ride along with his band."

"Safety in numbers."

"There's that, plus I don't want to get Winona mad at me if I take off with you before she has a chance to make her pitch."

Nate stared at the older man. "I really think you're exaggerating this out of all proportion."

"Much ado about nothing, eh?" Shakespeare retorted, and his shoulders shook with suppressed mirth.

Stung by his friend's baiting, Nate fell silent and thoughtfully watched the burial procession wind into the village.

Black Kettle was in the lead. The tall warrior halted

a dozen yards from his lodge and turned to address his people. For a minute he talked, and when he finished they dispersed to their respective lodges. Black Kettle came toward his guests.

"Be on your best behavior now," Shakespeare said in an aside to Nate. Then he straightened and stepped to meet the warrior, speaking in the Snake tongue.

Nate decided to occupy his time by reloading his pistols. He happened to glance at the crimson-coated rock the women had used as a chopping block, and his brow knit in confusion. How could anyone simply hack off a piece of finger as causally as he might pry a sliver from his skin? Did the gesture truly qualify as an act of sterling devotion, as Shakespeare maintained, or was the ritual another example of the crass behavior so typical of barbaric savages? He couldn't quite make up his mind one way or another.

And what should he make of this business concernng Winona? They hardly knew each other. The very idea that she might sincerely care for him was patently ridiculous. True, his heart seemed to flutter whenever he was in her presence, but his feelings could merely be confused physical attraction and nothing more. His one true love, Adeline Van Buren, was far off in New York City, awaiting his return. How could he even contemplate tarnishing her sterling memory by dwelling on the Shoshone maiden?

A sparkling voice spoke within inches of his left arm.

Startled, Nate looked up to find the lady in question regarding him quizzically. "Hello," he blurted out.

"Hello," Winona repeated precisely, and then indicated the pistol in his hand. Using sign language, she asked him to show her how to load the piece.

Feeling guilty over his line of thought and clearly self-conscious of her proximity to his person, Nate complied.

He patiently instructed her in how to check the vent leading from the pan to the barrel to ensure it wasn't blocked and would cause a misfire. With Winona brushing lightly against his arm, and distracting him terribly, he demonstrated the proper technique for measuring the charge of black powder. His nostrils detected a sweet scent emanating from her tresses as he showed her the way to hold the butt of the pistol against her hip with the muzzle slanted away from the body while doing the actual loading.

Winona appeared genuinely fascinated by the procedure. She was particularly interested in the means of inserting the patch and ball. Once, when his nervous thumb slipped as he tried to push the ball into the bore, she glanced at him knowingly and said a few soothing words in the Shoshone tongue.

Nate felt as if every square inch of his body was tingling by the time he finished his lesson. He tucked both pistols under his belt, hefted the Hawken, and stood as straight and true as his physique could accommodate.

Winona used sign to thank him, and also inquired if he would be staying the night.

Nate responded in the affirmative.

Smiling happily, Winona let him know she would be eager to talk with him later, then excused herself to go help her mother prepare the meal. She darted into her lodge, her long hair swirling, her lithe form moving with surpassing grace.

A lump had formed in Nate's throat. He swallowed hard and gazed out over the village, only to see Shakespeare eyeing him humorously. To his utter chagrin, Nate felt certain he inadvertently blushed. To cover his discomfiture, he pretended to be inordinately interested in a flock of startlings winging to the east. He heard footsteps and looked down.

"It's all settled," Shakespeare announced. "We'll stay

the night with Black Kettle, and at first light we're getting the hell out of here before the main body of Blackfeet show up.''

Hoping to avoid discussing Winona at all costs, Nate kept the conversation going. ''Do the dogs sleep outside at night?''

Shakespeare was surprised by the question. ''Yes. Why?''

Nate shrugged. ''I just wondered if they'd bother us, is all.''

The frontiersman's mouth twitched upward. ''No, the dogs won't bother us because we're sleeping in Black Kettle's lodge.''

''What?''

''When you're friends with an Indian, Nate, their home is your home. They'll give you the clothes off their back and the food off their table if you need it. When it comes to outright friendliness, the Indians have us whites beat all hollow.''

''Oh.''

Shakespeare nodded at three camp dogs standing ten feet away. ''Those mongrels stay out to keep watch. They'll bark like mad if anyone comes around.'' He laughed. ''They'd better bark. If a dog doesn't do its duty, it's usually eaten.''

The statement made Nate's head snap up. ''Will they serve dog at this feast we're attending?''

''They might,'' Shakespeare said, and had to turn away to conceal his merriment at the pained expression on his young associate.

''I can hardly wait,'' Nate said dryly.

The mountain man faced around. ''I wouldn't get too excited about the prospect. It's doubtful Black Kettle will serve us a prime dish like dog. That's for special occasions. Since I'm just like one of the family, we'll probably end up with deer or elk.'' He allowed himself to reflect the proper dregree of sorrow.

Nate brightened considerably. "I suppose I could make do with deer or elk meat. Besides, we wouldn't want to put them to any special bother on our account.''

"Perish the thought.''

"What should we do about our horses?" Nate inquired.

"We'll let them out to graze until dusk, then we'll tie them near the lodge for the night. You know the old saying. It's better to count ribs than tracks.''

Nate knew the saying. It referred to the fact horses were more likely to wander off or be stolen if they weren't secured for the night, and although the animals might put on a little weight by roaming and grazing, a wise horseman would rather count his mount's ribs in the morning than the tracks made during its nocturnal wanderings. "Do you mind if I ask you a question?"

"I can't promise I'll answer it, but go right ahead.''

"Do you have any close relatives back in the States?"

"Interesting question," Shakespeare commented, and glanced at Black Kettle's lodge. "Yep, as a matter of fact, I do. Two brothers and a sister. All three are doing quite fine. At least, they were the last I heard from them.''

"How long ago was that?"

"Seven years.''

"Isn't that a long time to go without hearing from your own relatives?" Nate queried.

"Not really. You may not have noticed, but I'm not a spring chicken any more. My kin and I pretty much parted ways about thirty years ago. If I make it back to Pennsylvania every ten years or so, I figure I'm doing okay.''

"Don't you miss them?"

"Every now and then. But I wouldn't have left if there hadn't been some serious problems we couldn't work out, and whenever I get to missing them I just remember how big a pain they could be,'' Shakespeare said.

''I don't know if I could go that long without seeing my family,'' Nate mentioned.

''That's something you have to settle to your own satisfaction. We're not all cut from the same cloth.''

Nate mulled those words as they engaged in casual conversation for the next 25 minutes. All the while as they conversed about the various Indian tribes and the rendezvous, he was thinking about his family and Adeline. How long could he abide being separated from them? When he'd first ventured west to St. Louis, he'd regarded the trip as a terrific adventure, a wonderful opportunity the likes of which he would never see again. But now he had already stayed in the wilderness for a lengthier period than he had dreamt would ever be the case, and the odds were that he would stay for quite a while longer.

Could he take the strain?

He'd told his folks and Adeline he would be gone for a year, but such an extended interval now seemed excessively long. Three months, yes. Maybe six months. But an entire year?

In due course Black Kettle emerged from the lodge and engaged Shakespeare in an animated discussion using sign language and the Shoshone tongue.

Nate understood snatches of their talk. They were merely swapping tales about their exploits since last they had seen one another. Black Kettle, apparently, had been in three battles with the Blackfeet, and the warrior expressed the opinion the Blackfeet were out to get him and had placed him near the top of their long list of enemies on whom they wanted to take revenge for past indignities they had suffered.

The mouth-watering aroma of cooking food wafted from the open lodge flap.

Nate smiled when he recognized the scent of deer meat. His mouth watered in anticipation, and he spent the next half-hour impatiently waiting for the meal to begin.

Finally an attractive woman who wore her hair in braids poked her head out of the doorway and said a few words.

Shakespeare looked at Nate. "Here we go. Now remember what I told you about your manners. If you become confused, just do like I do."

"I'll keep my eyes glued to you."

"I'll bet."

Black Kettle led them into the lodge and strode directly to his customary seat near the rear.

A cursory glance sufficed to show Nate that Winona was not anywhere in sight, and he repressed his disappointment while wondering where she could be. He dutifully followed Shakespeare around to the right, and they both paused while Black Kettle graciously indicated their seats on the warrior's left. Nate took his and studied the interior of the first lodge he had ever been inside.

At the very center, underneath the ventillation flap, was the cooking fire. A stack of firewood had been placed to the right of the doorway. To the left of the door, where they could be grabbed quickly in an emergency, were Black Kettle's weapons. The thick buffalo robes used for beds had been rolled up and positioned along the east wall. Personal effects were arranged along the west wall.

All in all, Nate was very favorably impressed. The cleanliness and warmth gave the dwelling a respectable, homey atmosphere he found quite appealing. His heart began to beat faster moments later when Winona entered the lodge and began assisting her mother in dispensing the food.

The meal turned out to be an education in itself.

To Nate's surprise, the first course was a large tin pan heaped high with boiled deer meat. He took a juicy chunk of venison, and the moment he did Winona placed a flat piece of bark in front of him to serve as his plate. He beamed at her, then leaned to his left and whispered to Shakespeare, "A tin pan?"

"Black Kettle picked it up in trade at the rendezvous last year," the mountain man explained. "Indians are real partial to our pots and pans."

Other courses were distributed. One consisted of a delicious flour pudding that had been prepared using dried fruit and the juice from various berries. After being mixed, the pudding had been boiled to the proper consistency and set to cool. Cakes and strong coffee were also passed out.

Nate saw Shakespeare draw his butcher knife and did the same. Eating utensils were restricted to knives and fingers, a practice Nate didn't mind in the least. He dug into his meal with gusto, surreptitiously watching Winona whenever he felt no one was looking.

Black Kettle and Shakespeare engaged in a running conversation during the entire meal. When they spoke in sign language, which they resorted to frequently, their greasy fingers fairly flew.

Nate tried to follow the gist of their discussion. He gathered they were talking about the general state of affairs in the region west of the Mississippi, but the particulars eluded him. He glanced at Black Kettle's wife a few times, noting her happy, contented expression, and heard her humming softly to herself while she worked. What did she have to be so gay about? he wondered. For that matter, Winona also seemed to be in exceptionally fine spirits. Why? Perhaps, he reasoned, they were overjoyed because they had been spared the ordeal of slicing off part of a finger. At the thought he gazed at the mother's hands and almost lost his appetite.

Black Kettle's wife had the tips of three fingers missing. Troubled, Nate chewed on a cake and took a swallow of hot coffee from a tin cup. He'd never understand the savage mentality. An elbow nudged him in the left side and he turned.

"Our host would like to talk to you," Shakespeare said. "I've told him that you're still trying to get the hang of sign, so he'll go slow. And I'll translate where necessary."

Nate deposited the rest of the cake on his plate and wiped his hands on his pants. He smiled at the warrior, keenly eager to make a favorable impression, and sensed Winona's eyes on him.

Black Kettle nodded and moved his hands and arms slowly, making a series of signs at a snail's pace.

Flooded with relief, Nate found he could understand the questions the warrior posed, queries concerning where Nate's parents lived, what Nate thought of the West, and whether or not Nate was married.

Shakespeare almost choked on his coffee at the last one.

Although he had to struggle to recall several of the signs he needed, Nate answered all of the questions adequately and honestly. He grinned, pleased at his performance.

Black Kettle then asked one more.

For a second Nate sat perfectly still, shocked, afraid he had interpreted correctly.

"Answer the man," Shakespeare prompted, a twinkle in his eyes. "Do you want to court his daughter or not?"

Chapter Ten

Nate was too flabbergasted to speak for a full 30 seconds. He glanced at Winona and saw her smiling at him expectantly, then looked at her father and inwardly recoiled at the warrior's stern visage.

"Cat got your tongue?" Shakespeare quipped, then became serious. "Remember what I told you about insulting an Indian."

Nate's emotions were swirling in a whirlpool of indecision. He wanted to say yes, but his memories of Adeline prompted him to decline. On the other hand, he certainly didn't want to offend Black Kettle or hurt Shakespeare's feelings, and he adopted the latter justification as the motivation for his answer. "Tell Black Kettle I find his daughter extremely attractive."

Grinning impishly, Shakespeare complied.

"Also explain to him that my knowledge of Indian ways is very limited. Let him know I'm unaware of the proper way to court an Indian maiden," Nate said slowly, selecting his words carefully.

Again the frontiersman translated.

Nate wasn't finished. "Tell him that for the white man

courtship can be a long, drawn-out affair. A man and a woman should get to know one another before they become involved.''

Shakespeare faced his companion. "You expect me to tell him that?"

"Yes," Nate declared. "And that I'm asking you to relay my words beause I want to be sure they are spoken perfectly. I respect him highly and would not want to accidentally insult him through my ignorance."

An appreciative smile creased Shakespeare's weathered visage. "You're a lot like your Uncle Zeke."

"I am?"

"Yep. You pack more wisdom between your ears than most men have in their little finger," Shakespeare said. He turned to the warrior and spoke at length.

Nate waited anxiously for Black Kettle's response. He studiously avoided gazing at Winona. What would his family think if they could see him now, discussing the courtship of an Indian woman with her father? His father and mother would probably throw a fit.

The warrior held forth next, speaking in a somber tone.

"He says he's not offended in the least," Shakespeare related. "In fact, he's pleased that you're so considerate of his feelings. He also believes a man and a woman should get to know each other. The Shoshones have a custom they adhere to in courtship, and he believes the custom will serve you well."

"What custom?"

Shakespeare twisted and pointed at a rolled-up buffalo robe lying against the side of the lodge. "A courting couple throw a robe over themselves for privacy and take a stroll in the moonlight."

"He wants me to take a stroll with Winona?" Nate asked, slightly shocked at the father's brazen attitude toward romance with his daughter.

"Whether you go or not is up to you," Shakespeare said. "All he's saying is you've got his permission."

Nate made the sign for "thank you" and indicated he would be delighted to walk with Winona.

Smiling contentedly, Black Kettle grunted and said several words to the frontiersman.

"What did he say?" Nate's curiosity impelled him to inquire.

Shakespeare smiled. "Why not now?"

"Now?"

"There's no time like the present."

"Just like that?"

Lines furrowed the mountain man's forehead. "What is the problem? You want to go walking with Winona. Go. Shoo!"

Nate started to rise, then hesitated.

"Now what's the matter?"

"I just had a thought."

"Uh-oh."

"We'll both be under the same buffalo robe, right?"

"That's the general idea. It's a bit difficult to get to know one another if you're under separate robes," Shakespeare quipped.

Nate saw Winona walk to the wall and pick up the rolled robe. He leaned toward his white-haired mentor. "What happens if I accidentally touch her?"

For a moment genuine astonishment caused Shakespeare's mouth to drop open, but he recovered and slapped his thigh in merriment.

"What's so funny?" Nate demanded uncomfortably.

"If you touch her, I doubt it'll be an accident," Shakespeare said, and cackled.

"You know what I mean. I don't want to be scalped for taking liberties with Black Kettle's daughter."

The frontiersman looked the younger man in the eyes. "Don't you know *anything* about women?"

"A little," Nate replied testily.

"Damn little," Shakespeare declared. "Now listen. No man can take liberties with a woman if she doesn't want them to be taken. Nine times out of ten it's the woman who fans the flames and in the bargain gives the man the mistaken notion that it was all his idea."

"But what about rape?"

Shakespeare blinked a few times. "Good Lord. You aren't fixing to rape her, are you?"

"Of course not."

"Rape is for weaklings. It's for men who don't have the gumption to face a woman in fair combat and lose honorably," Shakespeare said. "Now quit stalling."

"I'm not stalling."

"What would you call it? Babbling like an idiot?"

Nate slowly straightened.

"If it'll make you feel any better, no Indian woman has to stay under a buffalo robe if she doesn't want to," Shakespeare mentioned. "If you overstep yourself she'll just leave."

Winona stepped up to Nate and offered the robe.

Feeling as if he was moving in slow motion, a queasy feeling in his stomach, Nate took the robe and indicated the doorway.

Black Kettle addressed the mountain man, and received a response that made him burst out laughing.

"What did you say?" Nate asked.

"He wanted to know if you were ill. I told him you have water in your knees and mush between your ears," Shakespeare divulged, laughing.

"Thanks."

"Don't fret yourself. Romance has vanquished the mightiest of warriors."

"William S. again?"

"No. Me. Now get going before the sun comes up."

Nate motioned once again at the doorway, puzzled that

Winona hadn't already started outside.

"No, you dummy!" Shakepeare cautioned. 'Indian men always take the lead.''

"They do?"

"At least they think they do. Now go!"

Bowing graciously at Black Kettle and his wife, Nate backed toward the opening with Winona trailing him, a quizzical expression on her face.

Shakespeare gave a little wave and grinned. "This above all, young prince. To thine own self be true."

"What's that supposed to mean?" Nate asked, pausing near the flap.

"It means," Shakespeare answered, his eyes twinkling in their lined sockets, "you shouldn't light your wick until you can see the whites of her eyes." He threw back his head and convulsed in guffaws.

"The man is mad," Nate muttered, and exited the lodge. He halted in surprise at finding stars in the heavens and the sun long gone. A hand touched him lightly on the left shoulder. Inordinately startled, he turned.

Winona stood there calmly, her hands folded at her waist, her countenance most serious for someone about to go courting.

Nate smiled to reassure her, then proceeded to unwrap the robe, his fingers fumbling at the folds. To his consternation, he came across as a complete butterfingers. When the robe finally unfurled, inadvertently dragging in the dust before he could hold the hem aloft, he beckoned for her to step closer.

Obediently Winona took a short step and stood next to his left shoulder.

Mustering all the dignity at his disposal, Nate carefully draped the heavy robe over their shoulders. It covered both of them all the way down to their knees, screening them from public scrutiny, enshrouding them in a private domain of intimate proximity although they weren't actually touching. Nate found the experience discomfiting and oddly stimulating. He cleared his throat and held his head high, proud and self-assured.

Until he saw the warriors.

Nate froze when he beheld four young Shoshone warriors standing 20 feet away near a camp fire. They were all looking in his direction, and he wondered if they were upset because he was with Winona. He chided himself for leaving the Hawken in the lodge, but derived comfort from the fact he still had his pistols tucked under his belt.

One of the warriors suddenly came toward him.

Nate looked at Winona and smiled to reassure her that he would handle any situation, then placed his right hand on the corresponding flintlock.

The Shoshone, a tall warrior attired in a deerskin shirt and leggings, approached within a yard and halted. "Pardon," he said, his youthful voice betraying his age. "So sorry, Grizzly Killer."

Nate's surprise at hearing English spoken, even if in a halting fashion, was as nothing to his astonishment at being called by his Indian name. How did the warrior know? He remembered Shakespeare had told Black Kettle and a few of the other men, and the word must have spread through the village. "What do you want?" he demanded quickly to cover his embarrassment.

"My name Drags the Rope. Much happy meeting you."

A smile started to curl Nate's lips, but he caught himself and maintained a sober expression. Drags the Rope? What kind of name was that? His prudence overrode his curiosity and he asked a different question. "Where did you learn the white man's tongue?"

"Trapper Pete teach little. Six winters past."

"Well, I'm pleased to meet you," Nate said, uncertain

of the young warrior's motivation in introducing himself.

"Friend of Shoshones. Friend of Drags the Rope."

"I'll always regard the Shoshones as my friends," Nate stated, for want of anything better to say.

Drags the Rope nodded and smiled. "Much friend. Always remember." He turned and walked happily back to his companions.

Now what was that all about? Nate wondered, and shook his head. He'd said it once, and he'd wind up saying it a hundred times: There was no understanding the Indian.

Winona spoke a few words and nudged his shoulder.

Bothered by guilt over his train of thought, Nate stared at her and realized she wanted to walk to the east. He stepped off slowly, carefully keeping his hands clasped behind his back, keenly aware of her shoulder repeatedly brushing his.

They covered ten yards in silence.

Nate gazed idly at the nearby lodges, wishing he knew the proper words to say. For that matter, he would have settled for knowing *any* words in her language that could help him convey his feelings. "I don't know what to say to you," he stated aloud, hoping she would derive his meaning from the tone he used.

Winona answered, her words almost musical.

"I've never felt so helpless," Nate informed her, staring into her eyes.

Their shoulders came together and stayed together.

Nate had an urge to mop at his brow. The temperature under the buffalo robe seemed to have risen a good deal in mere moments. He coughed to clear his throat, thankful Shakespeare couldn't see him now. The mountain man would laugh himself silly.

Winona began talking and went on at great length, her animated expression compensating somewhat for her unintelligible vocabulary.

Entranced, Nate gazed at her lovely features and simply

drifted with the words, nodding at points he perceived to be appropriate and smiling broadly whenever she deigned to look at him. He scarcely noticed when they went past the last of the lodges and halted a dozen yards beyond.

Winona ceased speaking and turned to face him.

"Nice night," Nate said lamely, though truth to tell he hardly noticed the bright stars overhead or the cool breeze caressing his brow. The sum total of his personal universe was reflected in the beautiful countenance before him. Dim, flickering firelight cast her skin in a faint golden glow and put a gleam in her eyes. She smiled and her teeth sparkled.

They stood stock still for over a minute, their warm breath touching each other's lips.

"I can't believe I'm doing this," Nate declared at last. He thought of Adeline and the memory pained him. How could he betray her like this? With an Indian, no less. The thought gave him pause. Were those the words, or the words of a mindless Easterner, someone who had been conditioned to view Indians with a limited regard by society and his peers? Because in his heart of hearts he couldn't bring himself to think less of Winona simply because of her Indian lineage. At that moment, as their eyes exchanged silently the words they longed to voice, he regarded her as the most wondrous woman of any race.

Somehow they inched closer together until they were nearly touching.

Nate's senses were swimming. His blood pounded in his veins. He licked his dry lips, and suddenly the impossible occurred. Before he could quite control himself, before the fading remembrance of Adeline could interfere, all of Creation was rendered immobile by a singular act.

They kissed.

Chapter Eleven

"What the dickens did you do to that girl last night?"

Nate's head snapped around to his right and he glared at the frontiersman riding beside him. "Just what do you mean by that?" he demanded testily, and gave the pack horse a vigorous yank.

"Simmer down, for crying out loud," Shakespeare said, grinning. "I'm not prying into your personal affairs. But I couldn't help but notice the way she waltzed around this morning all smiles, humming and whistling to beat the band. The whole time she was helping to take down the lodge and pack for the trip—the whole blamed time—all that girl did was show teeth. I don't reckon I've ever seen anyone so happy about doing work in all my born days."

"You're making fun of me again."

"Wouldn't think of it," Shakespeare stated seriously, although the corners of his mouth twitched.

Nate shifted in his saddle and gazed back at the column of Shoshones trailing behind them. Most of the warriors stayed off to one side or the other, ever vigilant for an attack. Some of the women rode horses, but most walked with the children and dogs. Every lodge had been quickly dismantled at first light and secured to horses by means of a travois. Consisting of two lengthy poles tied crosswise behind the horse's head using stout buffalo tendons, then secured in position with strips of rawhide that were lashed to the lower sections to form platforms, the travois sufficed to transport almost every article the Indians owned. With slight modifications, such as circular cages constructed from thin branches that were affixed to the rawhide platforms, they could even be used to convey small children.

All infants were carried on the back of their mothers in ingenious devices known as cradleboards. Simplicity incarnate, each cradleboard was composed of a carved wooden frame that supported a soft pouch. Every cradleboard was different, designed and embellished according to the mother's whim. And every one was a study in versatility. They could be tied onto a saddle or hooked on a travois. They could be leaned against any other object when the mother needed her hands free. And in the lodge they were frequently hung on pegs or hooks. Unlike their white counterparts, an Indian infant was rarely placed flat. The cradleboards were invariably positioned upright, and as a consequence the infant did everything in the same posture they would use once they learned to walk.

Nate scanned the Shoshones in the column, searching for Winona. Nearly a hundred horses were used to move the camp. The larger lodges alone, like Black Kettle's, required upwards of a dozen animals. Earlier he had noticed an interesting aspect of the move, one that surprised him unduly simply because he never expected it.

The Indians were class-conscious.

Those Shoshones who were wealthier, who owned more possessions, who had the biggest lodges and more horses, led the move. Next came those with smaller lodges and fewer horses. And in the rear, choking on the dust stirred by those in the lead, walked the poorer wives with their two or three beasts of burden, including their dogs.

Winona walked near the front, engaged in guiding the horses pulling her father's lodge. She saw Nate glance at her, smiled, and gave a little wave.

"Yep. There she goes again," Shakespeare remarked. "Worst case I've ever seen."

Nate turned his attention to the mountain man. "I want you to know something."

"What, pray tell?"

"I intend to get even. I don't know how and I don't know when, but one of these days when you least expect it, I *will* get even."

Shakespeare chuckled. "Fair enough, Nate. I admire a man who has spunk."

Nate chuckled and gazed ahead at Black Kettle, Drags the Rope, and five other warriors who were 40 feet in front of the column. He thought of the tender moments he'd shared with Winona and sighed. "I need your advice," he stated bluntly.

"I figured as much."

"I really like Winona—" Nate began.

"Remind me to buy you a dictionary one of these days," Shakespeare interrupted.

"What? Why?"

"A man should always say what he means and mean what he says."

"Huh?"

"For you to say you like Winona is the same as a Shoshone saying he's not particularly fond of the Blackfeet."

"I don't see the connection," Nate said.

"Sure you do. You're just hoping no one else does, but you're only fooling yourself," Shakespeare stated.

"Will you advise me or not?" Nate asked indignantly.

"That's what I'm here for."

Nate stared idly at the winding valley they were following to the northwest, mulling how best to present his problem. He observed a raven off to the left, winging on the wind over an expanse of verdant forest. "All right. I won't beat around the bush any longer."

"I wouldn't want you to break a habit on my account."

"Please, Shakespeare," Nate said earnestly, looking at his companion.

The frontiersman promptly sobered. "Fair enough. Flat-out serious. What can I do for you?"

"I think I'm falling in love."

Shakespeare opened his mouth to reply, then changed his mind and simply nodded. "Go on."

"I've fallen head over heels for Winona, and for the life of me I can't figure out why," Nate related, and went on before the mountaineer could interrupt. "Hear me out. I have a beautiful woman waiting for me back in New York City. At least I hope she's waiting." He paused. "Or I *was* hoping, anyway, before I met Winona. And now all I do is think about Winona. I want to be near her all the time. But how can I become involved with Winona when my heart is in New York with Adeline?"

"Before you get in any deeper, let's clear up a few things," Shakespeare said. "I know how it is when a man is in love. His brain is all addled. Or, as old William S. would say, when the blood burns, how prodigal the soul lends the tongue vows. To put it straight, a man can't think straight. Which certainly explains your raving."

"Raving?"

"What else would you call it? The last I knew, it's not possible for a man to be in one place and his heart to go its merry way somewhere else. So your heart can't be in New York if you're becoming involved with Winona. Maybe your memory is still lodged in New York and tugging on your heartstrings, but I daresay your soul has succumbed to the lovely Winona's charms or I'm not the most cantankerous cuss in the Rockies.''

Nate nodded slowly. "What do I do?"

"What comes naturally.''

"That's not what I mean. How do I go about courting her without getting in over my head before I'm ready?"

Shakespeare chuckled. "It's a little late for that. You're already in over your head. If you didn't want to get involved, you should have declined to go for that walk last night.''

"But I didn't want to offend her father," Nate said quickly.

"Who are you trying to kid? I won't keep giving you my advice if you keep insulting my intelligence. Never label a gent as dumb just because he wears buckskins or wears his hair longer than you do. And always remember that experience has a way of sweating the fat from a brain, which must rate me one of the smartest men around what with all the gray hairs I've got.''

"Are you saying I'm committed to her whether I want to be or not?" Nate queried.

"You went and got her hopes all fired up, didn't you? You sweet-talked her and stood under the same robe with her. She made no secret of the fact she liked you, and you receiprocated. Now Winona naturally figures you and her are bound to be hitched before too long. Yeah, I'd say you're committed.''

"But I honestly don't know if I want to marry her.''

"It's a mite late to be putting the horse behind the cart, don't you think?"

"I don't know what to think," Nate said, and sighed. His emotions were in keen turmoil. On the one hand there was Adeline Van Buren, on the other Winona. On the one hand a woman who enjoyed a prominent social position and whose father possessed great wealth, on the other hand a woman who was a member of a wandering Indian tribe and whose father adorned the interior of his lodge with the scalps he had taken. They were as different as night from day, and he was caught in the middle. Correction. He had caught himself. Leaving a burning question in his mind. "What do I do?" he repeated softly.

"The decision is yours alone," Shakespeare commented, and stiffened in his saddle. He peered intently at the forest to the west.

Nate noticed and looked in the same direction. "What do you see?"

"I'm not sure," Shakespeare said, his forehead creased. "I thought I saw something move."

"What?" Nate asked, scanning the trees 30 yards distant. He failed to detect any motion whatsoever.

The frontiersman shook his head and started to relax. "Probably a deer or an elk."

"Why are you so jumpy?"

"Who's jumpy?"

"You are."

"I ate too much last night. I guess I'm still not over my indigestion."

Nate snorted. "Do you expect me to buy that? You have an iron gut. You told me so yourself."

"Believe a third of what you hear and half of what you see and you'll just about get the facts straight."

"Is that your motto?" Nate queried, grinning.

"You bet it—" Shakespeare began, and abruptly stopped, his gaze on the woods. He reined up and rested his right hand on the Hawken lying across his saddle. "Now I know I saw something."

Nate halted and stared into the shadows shrouding the base of the trees. He still saw nothing out of the ordinary.

"Let's take a look," Shakespeare proposed. He rode toward the forest without waiting for a response.

Puzzled by the mountain man's uncharacteristic nervousness, Nate quickly caught up, riding on his companion's right. In his right hand he held his rifle. He glanced to the northwest and saw Black Kettle and the other Shoshones had reined up and were watching intently. To his left the column of women, children, horses, and belongings still advanced.

"I could be making a fool of myself," Shakespeare remarked. "If so, it won't be the first time and I doubt it will be the last. But we can't afford to take any chances."

Twenty yards separated them from the treeline.

"Blackfeet, you think?" Nate asked.

"Some of that bunch got away yesterday, remember? I wouldn't put it past them to have gone after the rest of their war party, and then they swung around in front of us and set up an ambush."

"How would they know which direction we'd take?"

"They're not stupid. They've got to figure that Black Kettle's band is on the way to the rendezvous, and this is the shortest route," Shakespeare answered.

Nate looked at the woods. "I hope you're wrong."

"So do I."

But he wasn't.

Whooping and hollering, over three dozen Blackfeet emerged from concealment in the undergrowth. They waved their weapons in the air and broke into a gallop, heading straight for the column.

"We've got to turn them!" Shakespeare cried, and his white horse leaped to incercept the Blackfeet. "Leave our pack horse here!"

Winona was in danger! The thought spurred Nate to lash the reins and race even with the frontiersman. They angled to the left, listening to screams of alarm arising from the Shoshone women.

"They're going to try and drive off the horses!" Shakespeare shouted.

Nate nodded his understanding.

"And capture the women!" Shakespeare added.

Impulsively, Nate snapped the Hawken to his shoulder and took a bead on the foremost Blackfoot. He changed his mind at the last instant, preferring to save the shots for when he'd really need them.

The Shoshone women were trying to drive their animals to the east, away from the Blackfeet, while from all directions the Shoshone warriors converged on the column to protect their loved ones and property.

Nate hunched low in the saddle and the mare passed Shakespeare. He heard his name called but kept going. All he could think of was Winona, and his eyes strayed to the column where she was frantically striving to turn her father's horses. Attached to travois, and laden with lodge poles, robes, and overy other item the Indians owned, the animals awkwardly heeded commands and prodding. They were packed close together, and many collided in their incipient panic.

A Blackfoot armed with a lance broke away from the main body and rode directly toward Nate, yipping like a coyote.

Undaunted, Nate never slowed. The warrior was obviously trying to cut him off. He'd let the Blackfoot get nearer before firing.

Someone beat him to the punch.

A rifle cracked to his rear and the Blackfoot reacted as if kicked in the forehead by a mule, catapulting backwards, arms flung outward.

Shakespeare! Nate knew, and grinned in appreciation. His elation lasted only a few seconds, however, just long enough for him to draw within ten yards of the milling column. He'd managed to outdistance the Blackfeet, but only by 30 or 40 feet, and now five of them shrieked and whooped and bore down in a compact group straight at him.

Chapter Twelve

Nate risked a glance to check on Winona and found her still struggling with the horses. He also glimpsed Shoshone warriors rushing to the rescue from all directions, but none of them were close enough to prevent the Blackfeet from reaching the column. Then there was no time for anything except simply staying alive. The five enemy warriors were 20 feet distant when he lifted the Hawken, aimed, and sent a ball into the chest of the only one of the five armed with a bow.

The shot struck him just as the warrior drew back the string, and knocked him from his mount. Prematurely released, the arrow flew wild at a downward angle to the left and the shaft sank into the neck of the horse galloping alongside the archer's. The wounded animal whinnied in torment and shied to the right, colliding with a third horse in the process, slowing down two of the warriors.

But two more came on fast and furious.

No sooner had Nate fired the Hawken than he wedged the barrel under his left leg and drew both pistols, one in each hand. He cocked them, keeping them next to his waist.

The two Blackfeet pounded toward him. A war club graced the upraised hand of the warrior on the left while the second Blackfoot held a lance.

Nate met them head-on, deliberately choosing a course that would take him between the pair of bloodthirsty warriors. He waited as long as he dared to fire, until the Blackfoot holding the lance drew the weapon back and tensed to hurl it. Then he extended both arms, pointed a pistol at each warrior, and squeezed both triggers.

The twin cracks and the discharge of lead and smoke resulted in both Blackfeet falling to the hard ground without uttering a word or cry.

Gloating was out of the question.

The fourth Blackfoot, a husky man bearing a tomahawk, had gotten his animal under control after colliding with the injured horse, and he screeched an inarticulate challenge as he now raced forward.

All three of Nate's guns were empty and he couldn't hope to reload before the husky warrior reached him. He had no doubt the Blackfoot could wield that tomahawk proficiently, and the odds against him surviving were astronomical unless he could concoct a clever ruse.

Desperate straits called for desperate measures.

Nate sat tall in the saddle, gripping both pistols tightly. He saw the warrior draw the tomahawk back when they were a paltry 15 feet apart, and to counter the anticipated blow he did the totally unexpected. He leaned *toward* the onrushing Blackfoot and hurled his left pistol at the man's startled face.

The warrior instinctively ducked and twisted to the side.

Which was exactly the reaction Nate wanted. He closed in next to the Blackfoot's horse and swung the right pistol, clubbing the warrior on the bridge of his nose. Blood gushed and the Blackfoot reeled. Nate hit him again, on the mouth, splitting the warrior's lips and breaking off two front teeth.

The Blackfoot swayed and almost fell.

In a flash of inspiration, realizing he needed a suitable weapon for up-close combat, Nate lunged, grabbed the tomahawk handle in his left hand, and wrested the aboriginal hatchet from the warrior's grasp. Instantly he tucked his remaining pistol under his belt, transferred the tomahawk to his right hand, and swung with all his might.

Finely crafted, with a triangular metal head fashioned in a white man's forge and a red, factory-made cloth covering the handle, the tomahawk had apparently been received in trade from French traders hailing from Canada, with whom the Blackfeet were known to conduct an extensive business. The weapon possessed a perfect balance, and Nate found he could use it with ease.

The sharpened edge bit deep into the warrior's brow above the right eye, and the Blackfoot clutched at the handle as he vented a strained, gurgling gasp.

Nate tore the tomahawk free and swung again, aiming at the warrior's neck, and the edge cut into the soft flesh as if it were penetrating an overripe melon. Skin and muscle were readily severed, as were veins and arteries, and a crimson spray gushed from the fatal wound.

His eyes and mouth both wide in shock, the Blackfoot futilely pressed his hands over the gash, then sagged and toppled to the grass.

Nate hefted the bloody tomahawk, feeling a surge of confidence, and looked around for other foes. He didn't have far to look.

The warrior astride the animal with the arrow jutting from its neck was bearing down on him, the wounded horse gamely responding to its master's unspoken directions. The Blackfoot waved a war club and vented a challenging cry.

For Nate, there was barely time to turn the mare to meet

the attack. He swung the tomahawk as the war club descended toward his skull, and just managed to deflect the weapon. The blow jarred his arm all the way to the shoulder.

Instantly the warrior swung again.

Nate blocked the strike, and then was forced to do so again and again as the Blackfoot tried to connect with increasingly reckless swings. All about him he could hear gunfire, shouts, screams, and the neighs of horses, but he couldn't dare take his gaze from his opponent for even a second. In the back of his mind he wondered what had happened to Winona and Shakespeare, and he wanted very much to dispose of the warrior so he could aid them if necessary.

The Blackfoot had other notions.

Whipping the tomahawk in a hasty sideways parry, Nate battered yet another blow aside. For a moment his arm was extended and he was slightly off balance, and in that moment the Blackfoot revealed himself to be a seasoned veteran of many clashes.

Instead of swinging one more time in vain, the warrior vented a bloodcurling screech and launched his body into the air.

Nate tried to land a backhand strike and send his foe sprawling, but muscular arms wrapped around his shoulders and he was driven to the right with the Blackfoot on top. They were almost face to face as they dropped, and Nate looked into a pair of hate-filled eyes that implacably promised the most horrific fate imaginable if he should succumb to the designs of their owner. He came down hard on his right shoulder, felt the encircling arms let go, and rolled to his feet.

The Blackfoot was already erect and trying to plant a terrific swipe of his war club on the top of Nate's head.

Only a reflexive counter-swipe with the tomahawk saved

Nate from certain death. He deflected the club from his cranium, but the stone had struck a glancing blow off his left arm, causing excruciating pain and compelling him to retreat to avoid being hit again.

Sensing he had the edge, the warrior pressed his advantage, raining blows.

Nate blocked a half dozen in rapid succession, gritting his teeth against the agony in his arm, and racked his brains for a means of dispatching the Blackfoot quickly. There had to be something he could do, some ruse that would work! He inadvertently stumbled on a way a few seconds later when his right foot slipped and he fell onto his right knee.

Bellowing in triumph, the Blackfoot streaked the war club in a vicious arc.

Nate threw himself to the right, onto the ground, and felt the passage of air past his ear as the war club narrowly missed. For a second he was on his side within arm's reach of the warrior's legs, and without conscious deliberation on his part, exhibiting a savagery that surprised even him, he buried the tomahawk in his enemy's left foot.

The Blackfoot voiced a wavering screech and lurched backwards, striving to yank his foot free.

Nate tore the tomahawk loose and surged to his knees, drawing his right arm to the left as he rose, then swung. The edge ripped into the warrior's abdomen before the Blackfoot could retreat out of harm's way.

Uttering a visceral grunt, the warrior doubled over, his dark eyes the size of walnuts.

Without a pause, his lips set in a thin line, Nate jerked the tomahawk out. A loud squishing noise and a gasp from the Blackfoot attended the motion. He happened to look at the warrior's face and saw displayed there, not fear or capitulation, but raw, spiteful defiance.

Somewhere nearby a woman wailed.

Winona! Was it her? Eager to go to her aid, Nate slashed

the tomahawk across the warrior's throat. The razor-edged steel sliced the Indian's throat from side to side, and a crimson torrent sprayed out over Nate and the ground. He elevated his right arm to shield his eyes from the sticky liquid and pushed to his feet.

Wheezing and sputtering, the warrior sprawled forward. There was no time to lose!

Nate spun, scanning the battlefield, seeking Winona and noting the flow of the fight. The action had already passed him by, and the main body of Blackfeet had reached the column and were now engaged in brutal, fierce combat with the Shoshone defenders. The Shoshone warriors had rallied to defend their loved ones, and although out-numbered, they were acquitting themselves admirably, Black Kettle foremost among them. The Shoshone leader was in the thick of the conflict, wielding a war club like a man possessed, striking madly at every adversary within range.

The din was deafening. Whoops, shouts, screams, gunshots, whinnies, and the frenzied barking of the Shoshone dogs commingled in a cacophonous uproar. Dust clouds swirled into the air, obscuring portions of the valley.

There was no sign of Winona. No Shakespeare, for that matter.

Alarmed, Nate spied his mare standing 20 feet away and ran toward the animal. En route he reclaimed his rifle, which had fallen when the Blackfoot knocked him from his horse, and the pistol he had thrown. The latter he crammed under his belt, then slid the tomahawk next to it. Torn between his eagerness to participate in the combat and the realization that carrying three empty guns into a fight qualified as a prime example of sheer stupidity, he took the time to quickly reload the Hawken and one of the pistols, his fingers flying faster than they ever had. In slightly over a minute both guns were ready to go and he climbed on the mare.

The clash still raged.

Nate rode into the dust cloud, toward where he'd last seen Winona. He covered 15 yards without spying anyone, just horses and dogs, and then the dust abruptly cleared and he discovered a large party of Shoshones besieged by the Blackfeet. Four Shoshone warriors were battling seven Blackfeet, protecting a half-dozen women who were fleeting eastward while driving horses laden with travois ahead of them.

One of the women was Winona!

Even as Nate's gaze alighted on her, his blood seemed to chill at the sight of a Blackfoot who had singled her out and was trying to capture her.

Winona had a short pole in her hand. She was industriously swatting at the warrior in an attempt to drive him off, but her blows had only sufficed to make him angry.

Nate urged the mare toward them, his concern for Winona eclipsing all other considerations, even his own safety. He ignored everyone and everything except the struggle involving the woman whose lips tasted sweeter than the richest honey, whose embraces had promised so much the night before. An arrow whizzed past his head, but he paid scant heed.

Winona stood in danger.

All else was insignificant.

Neither of them saw Nate approach. He drew within two yards of the Blackfoot before the warrior awoke to his presence and turned. "Take this!" Nate cried, and extended the rifle barrel until the tip nearly touched the Indian's nose. He instantly fired, holding the Hawken in just his right hand.

The blast lifted the Blackfoot from his horse and propelled him over eight feet to crash onto the unyielding earth.

Nate almost went down himself. The recoil from the rifle, while negligible when the Hawken was held properly in both hands, almost tore the gun from his grasp, whipping his arm backward and rocking him in the saddle. He recovered, transferred the rifle to his left hand, and leaned down to offer his right arm to Winona. "Here!" he yelled. "Take my hand!"

She didn't understand his words, but his intent was clear, and she promptly took hold and allowed herself to be swung up behind him.

"Hold tight!" Nate advised, and pointed at his waist.

Winona nodded and banded her slim arms around his midriff.

Feeling strangely flushed, Nate wheeled the mare, about to speed Winona to safety far from the fight. He heard her cry out at the same moment he saw her father.

Forty feet to the west three Blackfeet had surrounded Black Kettle. He fought back valiantly, but they were clearly going to prevail unless he received assistance, and there were no other Shoshones close enough to lend a hand.

Winona shouted a word in Nate's ear and motioned at her father.

Did he really have any choice?

The question flickered across Nate's mind as he goaded the mare toward the unequal contest, drawing the loaded pistol and wishing he had taken the time to load both pistols.

Black Kettle had downed one of his opponents, bashing the man on the crown with a mighty swipe. As he twisted to confront the second Blackfoot, the third warrior, who held a slim lance, speared the shaft completely through Black Kettle's chest.

Winona screamed in terror.

Chapter Thirteen

Nate closed rapidly, cocking the pistol, filled with dread at the sight of thee Blackfoot yanking the lance out and Black Kettle pitching headfirst to the soil. Winona's arms tightened about his midsection, squeezing so hard it hurt.

The two Blackfeet weren't done with Black Kettle. The warrior holding the lance moved his horse next to the Shoshone's prone form and raised his arm for another thrust, evidently intending to be certain.

Winona sobbed.

Acting spontaneously, Nate pointed the pistol at the Blackfoot and at a distance of 25 feet squeezed the trigger. Much to his amazement, what with the range, the swaying of the mare, and the fact he had scarcely aimed, he scored.

The ball took the Blackfoot high in the right thigh, and in his shock and astonishment at being hit he dropped the lance.

At the retort the other warrior turned, a lean man holding a fusee. He took one look and raced off.

Nate stuck the pistol under his belt and drew the tomahawk, but the weapon wasn't needed. The injured Blackfoot reined his animal to the west and galloped away

without a backward glance. Nate was strongly tempted
to pursue the warrior and finish the man off, but he brought
the mare to a precipitate stop next to Black Kettle.

In a bound Winona was on the ground and kneeling
beside her father. She leaned down to inspect the hole.

Worried because they were in the open, exposed with
nowhere to take cover if they should be attacked, Nate
slid down and began loading the Hawken. He scanned their
immediate vicinity, taking stock of the situation.

The dust had pretty much dissipated. Bodies were in
evidence everywhere: men, women, children, horses, and
even dogs. Shoshone possessions were scattered in
profusion: lodge poles, many of them broken; buffalo
robes, torn and lying in the dirt; baskets and bowls and
blankets and dozens of items that had been crushed in the
general stampede to escape.

Nate spotted a large band of Blackfeet departing to the
east, taking scores of Shoshone horses with them. He saw
no sign of Blackfeet warriors nearby, and he deduced the
Shoshones must have driven the raiders off. A frantic
woman ran toward them from the southeast, and he
recognized her as Winona's mother.

Hoofbeats drummed to his rear.

Nate had just completed reloading. He whirled, bringing
the barrel up.

"Whoa, there, Grizzly Killer! I'm on your side,
remember?"

"Shakespeare!" Nate declared happily, overjoyed to
find the mountain man alive. He tempered his excitement
and stepped aside to reveal Black Kettle. "He took a
lance."

"Damn!" Shakespeare exclaimed angrily, and dropped
to the earth. He squatted next to Winona, examining the
wound for himself. "This is bad. Very bad. He needs
immediate medical attention."

Nate gestured at the retreating Blackfeet. "At least we won. We can give him the care he needs without fretting about them."

"That's where you're wrong, I'm afraid," Shakespeare said, looking up. "We're still in hot water."

"How so?"

"The Blackfeet will be back."

"They will?" Nate said, gazing after the war party.

At that moment Winona's mother reached them and sank down with a cry of anguish.

Shakespeare stood slowly, sorrow etching his craggy features. He stared eastward. "Those devils aren't about to let Black Kettle's band off the hook so easily. Unless I miss my guess, a third of his people are dead or dying."

"That many?" Nate stated in disbelief.

"And those bastards drove off almost all of the horses."

"Then why will they come back? They're already inflicted enough damage."

The frontiersman glanced at his companion. "Haven't you been paying attention? Indian warfare isn't like warfare among the whites. Rivals often fight until one side or the other is exterminated, even if it takes decades. At the very least they'll keep raiding each other until one side is driven hundreds of miles away." He paused. "The Blackfeet have been trying to kill Black Kettle for years. They want to wipe out his band, and they're not about to let this chance slip by."

Nate stared at the injured warrior, who lay unconscious with blood seeping from the cavity in his chest. "What do we do?"

"First we have to get everyone together, take stock, and see exactly how bad off we are. Then we've got to find a defensible position where we can hole up," Shakespeare said. He swung onto his white horse, looked at Winona's mother, and spoke several sentences in the Shoshone tongue.

The woman, whose normally stolid countenance radiated profound emotional misery, simply nodded in response.

Shakespeare glanced at Nate. ''Stay here with Black Kettle. Morning Dew and Winona are going to rig up a travois we can use as a stretcher. There's not much else we can do for him for the time being.'' He frowned. ''We've really got to get the hell out of here, pronto.'' So saying, he wheeled his mount and rode toward a group of five or six warriors 60 yards to the north.

Winona and her mother rose and hurried off.

So the mother's name was Morning Dew, Nate thought, realizing he had failed to inquire the night before. But then he had been rather preoccupied with musing about Winona. He studied Black Kettle for a minute, wondering if the warrior would live, noticing how shallowly the man breathed. The blood flow had reduced to a trickle. He could see the ring of pinkish flesh rimming the hole. Oddly, after all he had just been through, the sight made him squeamish and he quickly focused his attention elsewhere, watching the proceedings all about him.

Some of the Shoshones were going from body to body, ascertaining who was dead and who might only be injured. Others were industriously engaged in rounding up the scattered horses still in the vicinity, and a few were collecting undamaged personal items. The village dogs, temporarily left to their own devices, were lapping at puddles of blood, sniffing corpses, and to the south three of them were snapping at each other over which one would have the honor of tearing into a dead horse.

Nate used the opportunity to load both pistols and clean the tomahawk. The lethal effectiveness of the oversized hatchet had impressed him immensely and he decided to keep the weapon permanently. He tucked the handle under his belt at the small of his back where it was out of the way but handy in an emergency. What with the Hawken, the two flintlock pistols, the butcher knife, and the tomahawk, he was beginning to resemble a walking arsenal. He idly gazed northward.

Shakespeare had reached the group of warriors, five in number, and was addressing them. After a bit they spread out, going to their people and relaying instructions. One of the warriors turned out to be Drags the Rope.

A groan issued from Black Kettle's lips.

Nate glanced down, then over at the busy Shoshones, marveling at the rapport between the Indians and the mountain man. They appeared to trust Shakespeare implicitly and regarded his advice highly. This, despite the vast differences in their cultures and backgrounds. But was there really that great a difference? he speculated. If white men like Shakespeare could be so at home living as an Indian, if the frontiersmen who inhabited the wilderness could adopt Indian values so readily and be as much at ease experiencing life in the raw, were the differences between the whites and the Indians inherent or superficial? Or did the truth lie even deeper? Were some white men simply primitive at heart? Was that why they yielded to the call of the wild, as Shakespeare described it?

And what about his own feelings?

Nate had to admit that he found much to admire in Indian life, in the simplicity of existence they enjoyed and their affinity to Nature. He thought about life in New York City, about the hectic, frenetic, pace thousands upon thousands were caught up in each and every day, and he felt glad that he was out of that. All those years of contending with impolite people and carriage congestion, with overpriced goods and sooty air, seemed like the vague impressions of a bad dream. At least west of the Mississippi a man could set his own pace.

Provided he lived long enough.

Something touched his left leg.

Nate almost jumped out of his moccasins. He looked

at Black Kettle, shocked to find the warrior awake and gazing at him.

The Shoshone leader spoke a few words in his own language.

Shaking his head to signify he didn't comprehend, Nate squatted and scrutinized the area for Winona and Morning Dew, neither of whom were anywhere in sight.

Black Kettle coughed lightly and spoke again.

"Don't exert yourself," Nate said, and propped the rifle against his right shoulder so he could make the proper hand signs to tell the warrior not to talk.

Black Kettle motioned feebly, executing signs of his own, his hands barely moving.

"Must talk," Nate translated, and frowned. What could be so important that the warrior wouldn't lie still? Frustrated, he looked up and was relieved to spy his newly acquired friend from last night riding past 30 feet to the west. "Drags the Rope! Come here. I need you," he called out.

The young Shoshone warrior immediately turned his horse and hurried over. "Yes, friend Grizzly Killer?" he said as he slid to the ground. His eyes flicked to Black Kettle and he stiffened, then knelt and talked rapidly and softly in Shoshone.

Nate listened to Black Kettle reply, the words scarcely audible. He happened to glance to the southwest, and spotted Winona and Morning Dew over 150 yards distant. They appeared to be working at securing a travois to a brown horse they'd caught. He waved his arms overhead in an attempt to attract their attention, but neither one gazed in his direction.

"Black Kettle much words for you," Drags the Rope said.

Nate looked down. "For me?"

"Yes. Big words of heart."

"Are you sure he wouldn't rather talk to his wife or daughter? I can go fetch them."

Drags the Rope relayed the message to Black Kettle, who responded in a whisper. "No. Not wife. Not daughter. Words for your ears," the young warrior translated.

Perplexed, Nate squatted. "What could he possibly have to say to me?"

Again Drags the Rope passed on the question, and the answer he received clearly surprised him. He blinked, then stared at Nate. "Wants you take Winona."

"Take her where?"

"Wife her."

"What?" Nate asked in astonishment.

"So sorry. Wants you marry Winona."

"He said that!" Nate exclaimed, scrutinizing Black Kettle's inscrutable visage.

"Yes," Drags the Rope responded.

Black Kettle began speaking and went on at length.

"So much words," Drags the Rope stated uncertainly. "Hope speak rightly. My White Talk not best."

"What did he say?" Nate inquired apprehensively.

"Say he dying. Not long this world. Want know family fine before leave. Want you protect family."

"Me?"

"Yes. Want you marry Winna and have food and robes for Morning Dew."

"Food and robes?" Nate repeated in confusion.

"Yes. So sorry. Mean take care of her. Understand? Protect her. Take mother your lodge," Drags the Rope said.

Nate was at a loss for words. He cared for Winona unequivocally, but he wasn't ready to commit himself to her. Not in marriage anyway. Not until he knew her a lot better. But how could he tell that to a dying man?

Black Kettle talked to Drags the Rope, who then glanced at Nate. "Say you much like Winona, yes?"

"Yes," Nate admitted.

Drags the Rope relayed the word to the Shoshone leader and received more information to impart. "He say Winona like you much. Say you brave man. Say you be a good husband."

"But—" Nate began.

"Say Winona strong body. Much health. Have sons like bears. Many sons yours. She make good wife for warrior," Drags the Rope declared.

"I'm sure she would—" Nate began again, and was cut off a second time.

"Listen, please. Many words must say. I forget if not. Black Kettle know Shoshone warriors want marry Winona. Know many horses be his. But no need horses now. He want Winona happy, and she much want you. Much want. Understand?"

"I understand," Nate said, conscious of the leader's eyes on his face. He deliberately averted his gaze, troubled in his soul. Why didn't he just up and tell Black Kettle that he couldn't marry Winona at this time? He felt as if he was deceiving the man. Where was his courage? Why was he so tongue-tied? Could it be possible that deep, deep down he really liked the idea?

"Grizzly Killer?"

"What?" Nate snapped, forgetting himself.

"Something wrong?" Drags the Rope inquired.

"What could be wrong?"

"No idea. Black Kettle need answer. Need quick."

"An answer?" Nate said evasively, knowing the truth.

"Yes. Need know you will marry Winona. Please. Him not much time left. What say you?"

Nate shifted and locked his gaze on Black Kettle. He detected the fading expectancy in the warrior's eyes, and he intuitively perceived the critical importance of his response. The answer meant everything to the father and husband who would momentarily cast off his mortal shell and enter the vast unknown. Black Kettle wanted to die knowing his loved ones would be cared for, would be happy, and he was expending the last of his strength and energy while thinking only of Morning Dew and Winona. In light of so noble a sacrifice, Nate felt guilty about his own conflicting feelings.

How could he tell the man no?

How could he send Black Kettle into eternity in emotional distress?

Nate took a breath and voiced the single word that would link him indissolubly to the Shoshones and drastically alter all of his preconceived notions about his future, the momentous word that had changed more lives than any other in human history. "Yes."

Chapter Fourteen

"I can't leave you alone for two minutes."

"You would have done the same thing in my place."

"How do you know? It's risky trying to predict what another man will do in affairs of the heart because no two men are alike. I might have found a way out of it. I know I wouldn't have let myself be roped into a marriage I didn't want," Shakespeare stated testily.

Nate, in the act of arching his back to relieve a slight stiffness after three hours in the saddle, glanced at the frontiersman. "I don't see why you're so upset with me. You were the one who told me I was committed to Winona."

"Yeah, but I never claimed you had to up and agree to marry her out of pity."

"There's more to it than that."

"Oh?"

"I told you I think I'm falling in love with her," Nate reminded him.

"Getting married because you think you're in love is like wrestling a grizzly because you think you're bored and need a little excitement. In both cases a man winds up biting off more than he can chew."

"It's too late for me to change my mind," Nate stated.

"Black Kettle is still alive," Shakespeare pointed out.

"But for how long?" Nate countered, and twisted to survey the column behind them, a pale imitation of its former self. Where before there had been about a hundred horses laden with possessions, now there were 11 and all but two of them hauled injured Shoshones on makeshift hide platforms. Where before there had been almost 60 smiling, happy people, now there were 38 Indians, including those on the travois, and none were smiling or singing. Of that total, only nine were robust warriors capable of resisting another attack. Three of them trailed at the rear to cover the woman and children, while three rode on each side leaving Shakespeare and Nate to lead them to the northwest as swiftly as possible, which amounted to little better than a snail's pace. "I wish we could go faster," Nate remarked.

"We can't, not unless we don't care if some of the injured die on us," the frontiersman mentioned.

"I know." Nate stared ahead at a sloping hill they were slowly approaching. "What's your plan anyway? Other than putting as much distance as you can between us and the valley where we were attacked."

"That's it."

"You're kidding?"

"I wish I was. I know the Blackfeet will hit us again before nightfall, and I want to be ready for them."

"Maybe you're wrong," Nate said hopefully. "Maybe they were satisfied with killing twenty-two Shoshones and stealing all those horses." He tugged on the lead to their pack animal.

"They won't be satisfied."

"So you keep saying, but you don't know that for certain," Nate stated peevishly, annoyed that the mountain man kept harping on the worst likelihood.

Shakespeare sighed and looked at the strapping youth. "I know Mad Dog. He won't give up, believe me."

"Mad Dog?" Nate repeated, all attention.

"I recognized the Blackfoot bastard leading the war party," Shakespeare disclosed. "In his lifetime he's counted over eighty coup. Whites, Shoshones, Cheyennes, Arapahos, you name them, he hates them all. He had a run-in with Black Kettle about twelve years ago and came out on the losing end."

"Why didn't you tell me this before?"

Shakespeare shrugged. "I guess I didn't want you blabbing to Winona or Drags the Rope, although he might know. I think Black Kettle spotted Mad Dog, but he hasn't told anyone either. The Shoshones are brave, but the mere mention of Mad Dog's name would get them jumping at their own shadows."

"You're exaggerating."

"A little," Shakespeare conceded. "But the situation is bad enough without making it worse."

"So what can we do to stop this Mad Dog?"

"Pray."

Nate rode in silence for several minutes, pondering the information. One statement, in particular, galled him. "I'm not the blabbing type."

"I reckon I know that by now. My apologies then. I should have told you. But, if it's any excuse, you've got to admit I've been a mite busy and had a lot on my mind."

"You're forgiven," Nate said.

"Thanks," Shakespeare responded, and grinned. "Now I can sleep easier at night."

Nate looked over his left shoulder at Winona and Morning Dew, who were 15 feet behind him. The lovely woman he had agreed to marry mustered a wan smile. She was leading the horse pulling the travois on which her father rested. Beside the platform walked his prospective mother-in-law.

"I've been meaning to ask you something," Shakespeare mentioned.

"Ask."

The mountain man gestured at Nate's head. "What made you decide to wear it?"

Nate reached up and touched the eagle feather he had tied to the top of his head, at the back, using a short, thin strip of buckskin. He'd arranged the feather so that the flared end angled down and to the right, in the same fashion as several Indians he had seen. "I don't rightly know why I finally decided to put it on. Maybe because I was bored standing around with nothing to do while you were busy organizing our departure." He paused. "Or maybe it's because I think I have some idea now of the honor White Eagle bestowed on me."

Shakespeare nodded. "You're learning."

"Not fast enough to suit me."

"We have to take life at its own pace, Nate. Like the Good Book says, to everything there's a season, and a time to every purpose under the heaven."

"I don't believe it."

"What?"

"You quoted something besides Shakespeare."

The frontiersman made a show of slapping his forehead in feigned amazement. "Did I? I must have received a knock on the noggin and not realized it."

Nate chuckled and gazed up at the sun, which hung in the blue sky two hours above the midday position. "Will we stop before dark?"

"Not if I can help it. I don't care how tired the women and children become, they've got to push themselves to the limit. Once Mad Dog gets those horses he stole to a safe spot, he'll be back. Following our trail will be easy.

I expect he'll overtake us in no time."

"What about those graves the Shoshones buried their dead in?"

"What about them?"

"They weren't very deep. Will Mad Dog dig up the bodies to take the scalps?"

Shakespeare looked at his friend. "Indians might be a tad bloodthirsty, but they're not morbid. They don't go around digging up corpses just to take the hair."

"Oh."

"Where do you come up with some of these wild notions of yours?"

Nate ignored the question and scanned the hill they were starting to ascend. Trees dotted the northern and southern slopes, but the crown and the central portion were relatively barren except for a circle of boulders at the very top.

"It must be all those books you read back in New York," Shakespeare went on in the same lighthearted vein. "Books can give a person powerful strange ideas."

"Like the works of William Shakespeare?"

"Old William S. wrote about life, not strange stuff like some of those Eastern writers."

"Life, huh? Correct me if I'm wrong, but wasn't Shakespeare the one who wrote about witches, ghosts, fairies, and such?"

"Well, yes, but—"

"I rest my case."

The mountain man's eyes narrowed. "You're getting a bit too upity for your own good."

"I suppose I've been hanging around you too long."

They wound up the hill toward the summit, picking their way carefully around sections of the hillside where large, flat rocks covered the ground.

"This is interesting," Shakespeare remarked.

Why would a bunch of loose rocks hold any attraction? Nate wondered. He moved to one side and reined up, waiting for Winona to draw abreast of his position and thinking of the incredulous expression on her face earlier when Drags the Rope had informed her about her father's request. Black Kettle had passed out again by the time mother and daughter returned with the travois, and Drags the Rope had evidently gone into considerable detail in reporting the conversation he'd translated. Nate held up his left hand, recalling the warm pressure of her palm against his during that special moment when she had clasped his hands and turned to him the most wondrous countenance imaginable, a fascinating combination of affection and gratitude conveyed in an attitude of frank bewilderment, as if she couldn't quite believe that he cared for her and viewed his fondness as precious beyond words.

Shakespeare kept going. "We'll take a break at the top of this hill," he announced.

"Fair enough," Nate replied.

Winona drew nearer, firmly holding the horse's bridle, watching the animal's progress carefully to ensure her father wasn't unduly jostled.

Morning Dew walked with her head bowed sadly, her moist eyes fixed on her supine husband.

Would she cut off part of a finger if Black Kettle died? Nate speculated. An unbidden, similar question rocked his sensibilities. Would Winona hack off part of hers? The prospect disturbed him greatly. Traditional ritual or not, he didn't like the idea of Winona slicing a fingertip off, and he resolved to prevent her somehow if the problem arose.

Concentrating on the horse she led, the maiden had yet to notice he'd stopped.

"Winona," Nate said softly.

She glanced up in surprise, then beamed a weary smile.

"Hello, Nate King."

Nate enjoyed hearing her speak his name. From her clipped, perfect English, no one could have guessed those were the only three words she knew. He leaned down to pat the horse she led, then straightened and used sign to inform her they would be stopping on the summit. They rode upward side by side. Nate asked her how her father was faring.

Frowning, Winona made signs to indicate Black Kettle was on the verge of dying. Her mother had cleaned the wound and applied herbal treatments, but the lance had passed quite close to the heart and the probability of a complete recovery was extremely slim.

Nate commiserated as best he could, and apologized profusely for his inability to adequately communicate his ideas.

Winona told him that he was doing fine. She said she looked forward to learning his language and teaching him hers.

Engrossed in their sign exchange, they came to the crown of the hill.

Nate glanced up to find Shakespeare dismounted and inspecting the terrain. Right away he perceived the reason for the frontiersman's interest. The circle of large boulders, which were actually aligned more in the shape of a horseshoe, formed a marvelous natural fortification ideally suited to their needs. The boulders, on average about four feet in height, were spaced close together, the typical gap being not more than 18 inches. The open end of the horseshoe faced to the northwest, and the slope there was steeper than elsewhere. The eastern opening, through which they entered, was four feet wide.

Shakespeare motioned for Nate to join him.

"Take care of your father. I will be back," Nate signed to Winona, and dismounted. He stepped over to the grizzled mountaineer, whose eyes were twinkling.

"What do you think?" Shakespeare inquired.

"About what?"

"The lay of the land here. What else?"

"We can defend it easily," Nate said.

"That we could," Shakespeare stated, nodding as he surveyed the perimeter of stony sentinels. "We could hold out here indefinitely, if need be."

"We'd need water," Nate observed.

"Didn't you see it?"

"What?"

Shakespeare smiled. "Follow me." He walked to the row of boulders on the north and pointed.

Only then did Nate behold the pool of water lying between a pair of squat boulders. Partly camouflaged by the shadow cast by the left-hand slab, the pool measured two feet across and enclosed a third of the bottom of the right-hand rock. Only someone endowed with exceptional eyesight could have spotted it. "A spring, you think?"

"Looks that way," Shakespeare said, and knelt to dip his right hand into the water. "It's cold enough to be a spring." He reached in as far as he could. "And it's too deep to be rain runoff."

Nate scrutinized the clear space enclosed by the boulders. "We'd still need food."

"Horse meat is right tasty in an emergency."

"I don't get it. Why all this talk of staying here? I thought you want to put as much distance behind us as we can."

"I did," Shakespeare said. Before he could elaborate, shouts broke out from those climbing the east slope.

Nate spun, the Hawken clutched in his left hand. "What is it?"

"Mad Dog."

Chapter Fifteen

Nate ran past the boulders and halted on the slope. He gazed to the southeast and saw them, dozens of riders coming on hard perhaps a mile and a half distant.

"They'll be here in less than ten minutes," Shakespeare commented.

"So much for taking a break."

Drags the Rope and the eight other uninjured warriors rode up. "We go fight," the former announced. "Hold Blackfeet back. You get away. Take wives, take children."

"Don't be hasty, my friend," Shakespeare said.

"We not fight?"

"There's no reason to get yourselves needlessly killed. We have time to execute a plan I have in mind," Shakespeare stated, and launched into an extended speech in Shoshone.

Nate wished he could understand the tongue. He watched the women and children move hastily onto the summit. Off to the southeast the cloud of dust raised by the horses of the Blackfeet drew slowly closer and closer.

At last Shakespeare concluded, then changed to English again. "You know what to do. Get busy."

"You foxy, Carcajou," Drags the Rope said, smiling slyly, and spoke to two of the warriors. The pair immediately turned their mounts and raced down the hill.

"Where are they going?" Nate inquired.

"They're ̄our bait," Shakespeare answered, and chuckled.

Drags the Rope and the remaining warriors rode into the trees on the south side of the hill.

"Are they bait too?" Nate asked.

"They're gathering branches for our breastwork."

"You have this all worked out, don't you?"

"In matters of life and death it doesn't pay to dawdle," Shakespeare remarked, and returned to their natural fort. He began issuing instructions to the Shoshone women and children, who galvanized into action, with as much alacrity as if he had been one of their own.

What if he was? Nate wondered. He'd heard tell that certain tribes adopted white men into their midst, and he had never thought to ask if the Shoshones had adopted Shakespeare. Glancing once more at the dust cloud and the two warriors galloping toward it, he hefted his rifle and went into the area enclosed by the boulders.

The women and older children were busily at work in erecting a crude but creditable breastwork across the opening to the northwest, using brush, manageable stone, and logs. They left a three-foot gap in the center.

Shortly the warriors with Drags the Rope returned, dragging stout limbs. These were passed to the women and placed at appropriate points in the breastwork.

Other children herded the animals to the middle of the cleared space, which encompassed 60 feet from one side to the other, and went around tying the mouths of the dogs shut so the canines couldn't bark.

Nate walked over to Winona and Morning Dew, who were standing next to Black Kettle's travois located near the spring. Both women looked at him expectantly.

"Are we making a stand?" Winona signed.

Nate responded in sign language, advising her they were indeed preparing to fight Mad Dog.

Mother and daughter exchanged startled glances, and it was Morning Dew who addressed him next, her hands and fingers flying almost too rapidly for him to follow.

Instantly Nate realized his mistake. He'd gone and done exactly what Shakespeare had been afraid he'd do. Morning Dew wanted to know how he knew Mad Dog led the Blackfeet. She demanded to be told why no one had informed her. Was the news a secret the men were keeping to themselves? He saw anger in her eyes, and he wanted to go over and beat his head against one of the boulders just so he could knock some sense into his skull.

"Don't tell me," a gruff voice stated sternly to his rear.

His face a study in embarrassment, Nate pivoted. "I'm afraid I'm the blabbing type after all."

Shakespeare shrugged. "Oh, well. Can't be helped. I reckon it's time they knew anyway." He spoke to the women in their own language for a minute.

"There's something I'd like to know," Nate stated when the frontiersman fell silent.

"What is it?"

"Why are the Shoshones following your instructions? Why aren't they listening to one of their own warriors?"

Shakespeare nodded at Black Kettle. "Because the best warrior in this band is out of commission, and Drags the Rope and the others know that I have experience along these lines." He paused to regard the progress of the breastwork. "Let me fill you in on a secret, Nate. When it comes to one-on-one combat, Indians are able to hold thier own against anyone. But in general warfare they're not much for taking directions. They don't organize their attacks very well. A war chief might lead a raid, might lead the first assault, but after that it's every man for himself. They usually rely more on speed and force of numbers than strategy.''

''Which still doesn't explain the reason they're listening to you.''

''They trust me. I've lived among them off and on for years. They know I won't let them down,'' Shakespeare answered. ''And too, they know there isn't time for them to squabble over the best tactics to use.''

''Maybe they should make you their chief,'' Nate joked.

''I wouldn't accept the job.''

''Why not?''

''Because I can't stand being tied down to any one place for very long. A chief has to stay with his people, to be there when they need him, to settle all the petty problems that crop up, to always be at their beck and call.'' Shakespeare shook his head. ''That kind of life isn't for me, thank you very much.''

Drags the Rope and the other warriors came over. They promptly dismounted and began checking their weapons: testing bow strings, verifying rifles were loaded, and loosening knives in their sheaths.

Shakespeare nudged Nate and pointed at the boulders rimming the east side of the hill. ''Would you keep your eyes peeled for the two men we sent as decoys? I'm going to lend a hand with the breastwork.''

''Sure,'' Nate said, and strolled over to the perimeter. He placed the Hawken on the flat top of a three-foot-high slab and leaned on the edge.

Approximately a mile off were the Blackfeet, still riding at a fast pace, sticking to the trail the Shoshones had made.

Nate began to speculate on whether he would ever reach the rendezvous. He would never desert Winona, and because of her his fate was inextricably bound to the whole band. A keen admiration for his hoary companion filled his heart. Shakespeare could leave any time he wanted, and yet the man had decided to stick with the Shoshones through thick and thin. The man had grit.

A golden eagle materialized to the south, flying from east to west.

Nate idly watched the big bird of prey and thought of the eagle feather in his hair, which belonged to a bald eagle, not the golden variety. How did the Indians obtain the feathers? He'd lost track of the number of warriors he'd seen who adorned their hair or shields or whatever with such feathers. They certainly couldn't collect so many feathers from birds that had died natural deaths. Did the Indians kill eagles? Or perhaps trap them? He decided he would ask Shakespeare when the right opportunity presented itself.

Mad Dog and his war party were continuing their steady advance.

It was funny, Nate mused. Here he was, intimately involved with a band of nomadic Plains Indians, prepared to give his all, if necessary, in their defense. Yet a year ago, even six months ago, he'd seldom given Indians more than a passing thought. When he had lived in New York City, in the throbbing hub of a mighty nation, surrounded by all the comforts and culture the metropolis had to offer, able to meet all of his needs by the flip of a coin or the exchange of a few bills, he'd never seriously pondered that fact that a thousand miles away dwelt hundreds of thousands of people who lived hand to mouth, who were dependent on the cycle of Nature for their existence, who went hungry when the game was scarce and thirsty during a drought, who knew no such constraints as those often meaningless rules and laws imposed on their so-called civilized counterparts, who roamed as free as the first man, Adam, must have been in the Garden of Eden.

There was that word again.

Freedom.

Many times he had asked himself why white men would

be willing to tolerate the hardships of the wilderness when life was so much easier back in the States. The answer became increasingly more apparent the longer he dwelled in the West.

Freedom.

For a man or woman to be able to live as they saw fit without harming others, to be able to put food on the table through their own efforts with a gun or a hoe, to be able to fabricate their own clothing and construct their own homes without having to rely on anyone else, to be totally self-sufficient, seemed to him to be the ideal way of living. The realization made him chuckle. He was thinking more and more like Shakespeare every day.

The Blackfeet were now three-quarters of a mile distant.

Nate gazed over his shoulder at the defensive preparations. Exercising remarkable zeal, the Shoshones had hastily erected the breastwork to a height of four feet. The women were ushering all of the children to the middle, where the men were already occupied in compelling each and every horse to lay down.

Now why were they doing that?

Shakespeare came toward him. "What's the status on those murdering savages?"

"They'll be here soon enough," Nate said.

"Good," Shakespeare declared, and grinned wickedly. "We'll have a little surprise for them."

"Aren't you taking a big risk?"

"Would you rather have Mad Dog overtake us somewhere else? Somewhere he'd have the advantage?"

"No," Nate admitted.

"Then this is where we'll make our stand," Shakespeare stated, halting next to a boulder on the left. "With any luck we'll give them such a licking they'll head for the hills and leave us alone."

"I hope you're right."

"Most Indians aren't fanatics about dying," Shakespeare mentioned. "When a battle goes against them, when there's no point to be made by needlessly wasting lives, they head for home."

"What about this Mad Dog? Is he a fanatic?"

"As loco as they come."

"How'd he ever get such a name, anyway?"

The frontiersman stared at the Blackfeet. "I heard tell he took it after a run-in with a rabid mutt."

"He took his own name?"

"It happens all the time. Indian babies are given their names right after birth. Sometimes they're named after animals, sometimes for something connected with nature that occurs the day they're born, like a thunderstorm, or else they get their name from a physical deformity they might have. Usually the women keep theirs throughout their lifetime, but the men often change the name they were given when they count their first coup, commit a brave act, have a vidid dream, or tangle with a wild beast."

"Like a mad dog?"

"Or a grizzly bear," Shakespeare said with a grin.

"And they even bestow such names on us," Nate commented thoughtfully, reflecting on the honor White Eagle had extended to him by giving him the name Grizzly Killer. The more he learned concerning Indian beliefs, the more he grew to value the singular distinction. He stared at the Shoshone warriors. "Why would a man take a name like Drags the Rope?"

Shakespeare chuckled. "Don't let the name fool you. He got it from one of the bravest acts I've ever seen."

"You were there?"

"Yep. About three winters ago," Shakespeare said, then corrected himself. "Sorry. Three years ago. It was during a buffalo surround."

"A what?"

"Indians have several ways of taking large number of buffalos. One of the tricks they use is for a lot of warriors to ride out on the plains, fan out around a herd, and drive all the animals into a circle. Then they take to killing the critters as fast as they can. It's damned dangerous work, though, because the buffalo, particularly the big bulls, will lash out with their horns and try to gore the horses and riders.''

Nate had hunted buffalo with his uncle, and he could envision the scene Shakespeare depicted. "You'll never catch me hunting buffalo that way."

"It's not for the faint of heart. The Indians have to get in close with their lances or bows to make the kill. Three years ago Drags the Rope was on a surround. One of his friends got knocked to the ground when a bull gutted the man's horse. That ornery bull would have gored the friend too, if not for Drags the Rope. He had a rope with him because he was planning to haul one of the cows he'd killed back to the camp for a feast. When he saw his friend go down, naturally he rode in to help. He'd thrown his lance into another buffalo and had no way to turn the bull except with the rope. So he started waving the rope in front of the bull, dragging it on the ground behind his horse and swinging it from side to side to get the bull's attention," Shakespeare detailed. "And you know what? It worked. That fool bull took off after the rope. Trailed after Drags the Rope for hundreds of yards. Almost got his horse too. Finally another brave shot the thing. But if not for Drags the Rope's bravery, his friend surely would have died.''

"And that's how he acquired his name," Nate said.

Shakespeare nodded. "Some Indian names might sound funny to you, but there's always a good reason for every name given."

At that moment the warrior in question joined them, accompanied by the other Shoshone men. "We ready fight," he announced boldly.

"Good," Shakespeare responded, facing eastward. "Because here come your enemies."

Chapter Sixteen

Mad Dog and the war party were only a quarter of a mile from the hill.

"Do you think they know we're here?" Nate asked.

"Not yet," Shakespeare said, and motioned for everyone to take cover behind the boulders.

Nate ducked down and peered at the valley below. The Blackfeet were coming up the center, following the tracks of the Shoshones. Bordering the valley on both sides was forest. "Where are your decoys?" he queried.

"Right there!" Shakespeare exclaimed, jabbing his right hand at a stretch of woods two hundred yards from the base of the hill.

Nate saw them. The pair of warriors broke from the trees and raced toward the hill, seemingly fleeing for their lives, their bodies hunched low over the backs of their mounts.

Instantly the Blackfeet voiced a collective whoop and took off in pursuit, waving their weapons in the air as they goaded their animals to top speed.

"Now we'll see how bright Mad Dog is," Shakespeare stated. "If he takes the bait, he'll pay."

Nate took hold of the Hawken in both hands and

nervously stroked the hammer. "Do we wait to fire until we can see the whites of their eyes?" he joked.

"Yep."

"You're kidding."

"Nope. I want those bastards so close that we can see the sweat on their skin," Shakespeare said.

"But they outnumber us. How can we prevent them from overrunning our position if they're that close?"

"We shoot staight."

Nate didn't like the idea of permitting the Blackfeet to get very near to the fortification. He preferred to pick them off from long range. If the Blackfeet were ever able to breach the defenses and run amok within the circle of boulders, the poor Shoshones wouldn't stand a prayer.

Below the hill the race continued. With a six-hundred-foot lead on the Blackfeet, the two Shoshone warriors were easily holding their own. Mad Dog and his band screeched and vainly endeavored to narrow the range.

Nate glanced at the Shoshones crouched to his right and left. One held a rifle, five had bows, and one was armed with a lance. He remembered the information the mountain man had imparted about the accuracy of Indian archers, and he hoped it applied equally to the Shoshones.

A gunshot cracked in the valley.

Instinctively elevating the Hawken to his right shoulder, Nate looked down and deduced that one of the Blackfeet had foolishly fired and missed.

The pair of Shoshones were almost to the bottom of the hill.

"Remember, don't squeeze the trigger until I do," Shakespeare advised Nate, then repeated the order in the Shoshone language.

An air of tense expectancy gripped the defenders.

Although simmering with excitement inside, Nate casually glanced at the women and children huddled to his rear. Winona had her eyes on him and he smiled to express his reassurance that all would go well. Morning Dew was leaning over Black Kettle, apparently tending to his wound again. The children, horses, and dogs were all quiet, and he marveled at how disciplined the youngsters were, even the infants. Not one of them cried. Evidently the lessons the mothers imparted to instill obedience worked wonders.

The men acting as decoys were galloping up the slope.

"If you spot a Blackfoot wearing a dark beaver hat, that'll be Mad Dog," Shakespeare disclosed. "Don't hesitate to put a ball through him."

"I haven't seen many Indians wearing hats," Nate mentioned while watching the Blackfeet advance.

"A few are right partial to the hats white men wear," Shakespeare said conversationally, as if they didn't have a care in the world and weren't about to battle a band of bloodthirsty warriors. "I knew a Sioux once who took to wearing a top hat and a fancy coat. By the same token, there are white men who have gone over totally to the Indian way of living. They go around buck naked or wear only a breechcloth." He paused. "Never could see the sense in that. Had a spooked horse take me through a brier patch once. Just think what would have happened if I wasn't wearing clothes!"

Nate glanced at the frontiersman, amazed at his friend's easygoing attitude when they were literally staring death in the face. "I want you to know I've enjoyed our time together."

Shakespeare studied the younger man for a moment. "Don't be talking like that. We're not dead yet. And just between you and me, I have no intention of dying for another twenty or thirty years. When the Grim Reaper comes for Old Shakespeare McNair, he's going to have a tussle on his hands."

A pounding of hoofs heralded the arrival of the two decoys, who swept through the opening in the eastern line of boulders and abruptly reined up. They slid to the ground as two women came forward to take their perspiring animals. Doubling in half, the two men united with their fellows and crouched in the shelter of separate rocks.

Nate peeked over the top edge of the boulder and nervously licked his dry lips when he spied the Blackfeet starting up the hill. Quickly he conducted a count and pegged the tally at 31. Thirty one! Three times as many as the combined defending force!

"Hold your fire," Shakespeare directed, then repeated the command to the Shoshones.

Easy for him to say! Nate thought, nervously fingering the trigger. It took all of his self-control to refrain from leaping up and snapping off a hasty shot as the war party thundered ever closer to the crown. So intent were the Blackfeet on catching the decoys that they were uncharacteristically careless, goading their horses up the grade without pausing to survey the top.

Shakespeare chuckled. "I've always maintained that the Blackfeet sit on their brains," he quipped, and became serious. "Get ready."

"I'm as ready as I'll ever be," Nate muttered, and the act of speaking alleviated his tension somewhat.

The onrushing Blackfeet were now one hundred feet from the fortification, and the boulders, combined with the angle of the slope, prevented them from seeing the concealed Shoshones and animals.

"Where the dickens is Mad Dog?" Shakespeare asked, scanning the attackers intently.

Nate noticed a lot of bows and fusees in evidence.

Still whooping and hollering madly, the band raced higher. Only 80 feet remained to be covered.

Nate cocked the Hawken and heard a click as

Shakespeare did likewise.

The distance narrowed to 70 feet.

"Say, Nate," Shakespeare said.

"Yeah?" Nate responded without taking his eyes off the charging Blackfeet.

"It's too bad your Uncle Zeke went under. He'd be right proud of you if he could see how you've taken to life out here. He told me once that you were the only one of his relatives who was worth a damn."

Surprise almost caused Nate to glance at the mountain man, but he steeled his will and concentrated on their enemies. Why did Shakespeare mention such a fact at a time like this? he asked himself. And then there was no time left for idle reflection.

Forty feet of ground separated the two forces.

Thirty feet.

A mere 25.

"Give them hell!" Shakespeare bellowed, and rose from hiding with his rifle pressed to his right shoulder.

Nate stood and snapped the Hawken up. For a moment he had the impression a horde of Indians filled the slope. Astonishment rippled from visage to visage. He sighted on a warrior directly in front of him and squeezed the trigger. The blasting of the rifle and the Blackfoot toppling from his horse were nearly simultaneous.

Shakespeare's rifle boomed and another warrior went down.

The Shoshones were firing arrows as swiftly as they could notch their shafts and pull back their bow strings.

Taken completely unawares by the ambush, the Blackfeet lost eight of their men in the opening seconds of the conflict to well-placed balls or arrows. Two others were gravely wounded. Panic seized the majority, and they brought their animals to a sudden halt and attempted to turn their mounts and flee. Packed close together, their frantic efforts resulted in general confusion. Horses collided, men shouted and cursed, and dust swirled into the air.

Not all of the Blackfeet tried to retreat.

A pair of Warriors came straight for the boulders, each firing a bow.

Nate recoiled in alarm as a shaft buzzed past his head. He set down the Hawken and drew both pistols, but before he could fire someone else disposed of the duo.

Drags the Rope stepped into the wide opening, blocking the path of the pair, an arrow already fitted to his bow string. He aimed at one of the Blackfeet, who was drawing back a shaft, and let fly. His slim missile leaped to meet his foe, and the point ripped into the Blackfoot's throat.

Flinging his arms outward, the enemy fell.

Drags the Rope stayed rooted to the spot, his right hand flying as he swept a shaft from his quiver and placed the notch to the string.

The second Blackfoot loosed an arrow.

Unperturbed and unflinching, Drags the Rope was sighting along his shaft when the Blackfoot's arrow creased his left shoulder blade, gouging a shallow furrow in his skin but not imbedding itself in his flesh. His features shifted and hardened and he fired.

In the act of whipping another arrow from his quiver, the Blackfoot flew backwards when the tip penetrated his left eye and bored out the top of his cranium.

Nate glimpsed the exchange as he leveled both pistols at an adversary endeavoring to gain control of a recalcitrant animal. He squeezed off a shot from his right flintlock.

The ball hit the Blackfoot high on the left shoulder, passed through the fleshy part of his arm, and tore into his chest, drilling through his lungs before it came to a stop when it lodged against a lower rib bone. Twisting and clutching at his side, the warrior pitched forward.

One of the Shoshones darted from cover, a lance held in his right hand. He ran straight toward a Blackfoot and pumped his arm back for the toss.

Reacting instantaneously, the Blackfoot fired a fusee.

Nate saw the Shoshone's head snap around as the ball took him squarely in the forehead. He extended his left flintlock and sent a return shot into the Blackfoot's torso.

Having finally succeeded in disentangling themselves, the Blackfeet were beating a hurried retreat down the east slope. They cut to the right at the bottom and made for the nearest trees. A few shook their fists at the crest and uttered inaudible oaths.

The Shoshone warriors stepped into the open and voiced yips of delight at their victory, shaking their weapons overhead in triumph.

"Damn! We did it!" Shakespeare declared.

Nodding grimly, Nate surveyed the carnage. He counted 15 Blackfeet littering the ground, which meant there were 16 still alive. An improvement over the previous odds, but the defenders were still outnumberd. He glanced at the Shoshone who had been shot through the head, then glanced to his left and spotted another one lying flat on the earth with an arrow jutting skyward, its point apparently sunk in the warrior's heart. So there were nine left, including Shakespeare and himself.

"You don't look very happy," the mountain man observed.

"We're still outnumbered."

"True, but we gave those bastards a taste of their own medicine. They may change their minds about taking our scalps and head for home."

Nate looked at him. "Do you really believe that?"

A wry smile creased the frontiersman's lips. "No, but a man can always hope, can't he?"

"I didn't see Mad Dog," Nate commented as he began

reloading his guns.

"I spied the son of a bitch in the pack, but I couldn't get a bead on him," Shakespeare lamented.

"Do you think he got away?"

"Let's go check," Shakespeare proposed. "But first . . ." He clasped his powder-horn and proceeded to reload his rifle.

At least half of the downed Blackfeet were groaning in pain. Several were attempting to stand or crawl off. One stocky warrior, an arrow transfixing his neck from side to side, had risen to his knees and was bent over, coughing up blood.

"Let's finish those buggers off," Shakespeare suggested.

Four Shoshones had the same idea. They moved among the fallen, plunging their knives repeatedly into prone bodies until satisfied their foes were definitely dead.

Nate wedged his pistols under his belt and picked up his rifle. He gazed to the south at the forest but saw no sign of the Blackfeet. A commotion erupted on the slope and he spun.

A Shoshone had leaned down to plunge his knife into a Blackfoot, who had been lying face down, and when he gripped the Blackfoot's shoulder the man suddenly flipped over and buried a knife of his own in the Shoshone's groin. In a twinkling the Blackfoot stabbed the Shoshone twice more.

Shakespeare's rifle spoke.

The Blackfoot grunted as the ball punctured the base of his throat and he collapsed again, blood spurting from the cavity. He breathed in great, ragged gasps.

A trio of Shoshones pounced on the culprit and dispatched him with a series of blows, rendering his chest a pincushion for their blades. The Blackfoot's legs convulsed for a bit, then he was still.

Shakespeare ran to the Shoshone who had been stabbed and knelt down to examine him.

Warily watching the trees, Nate followed.

"He's done for," the frontiersman stated in disgust.

That leaves eight, Nate thought, and glanced at the Blackfoot transfixed by the arrow just as the warrior surged erect and bounded forward, a war club held in his upraised right hand.

Chapter Seventeen

Nate would have snapped off a shot while holding the Hawken at waist level, and he probably would have scored a hit at such close range, but Shakespeare suddenly stood, blocking his view of the Blackfoot and preventing him from firing.

The mountain man was straightening to his full height, his rifle coming up, when the unforeseen transpired. His left moccasin slipped on a slick spot of blood and his left foot buckled, sending him stumbling rearward.

Nate tried to sidestep, but Shakespeare slammed into him and knocked him to the right.

Before either man could recover his balance, the Blackfoot reached them and swung. Descending in a short, vicious arc, the war club connected, sriking the frontiersman on the left side of his chest as he tried to maintain his footing.

Shakespeare went down.

And at last Nate had a clear field of fire. He stopped stumbling, pointed the barrel at the Blackfoot, and got off a hurried shot that nailed the warrior full in the mouth and burst out the back of the Indian's cranium. The impact lifted the Blackfoot from his feet and propelled him a yard to crash onto a corpse. Nate whirled toward the mountain man. "Shakespeare!" he cried.

The grizzled frontiersman lay on his right side, blood seeping from the ragged tear in his buckskin shirt where the sharp stone head of the war club had connected. His rifle was beside him. Wincing, he looked up and shook his head. "Pitiful. I must be slowing down. Ten years ago he never would have touched me."

"Don't talk," Nate instructed him, kneeling. "Let me have a look at it."

"Just a scratch," Shakespeare mumbled.

"I'll be the judge of how severe it is," Nate admonished.

Drags the Rope and four of the warriors clustered around the mountain man. "Carcajou die?" asked the tall Shoshone.

"No, I'm not dying, you busybody," Shakespeare snapped. "It's just a damn scratch, is all."

"I told you not to talk," Nate said, and glanced at Drags the Rope. "Check the rest of the Blackfeet. Finish them off. But be careful! We can't afford to lose another man."

"We careful," Drags the Rope promised. He turned to go.

"Have someone keep an eye on those trees," Nate added. "The Blackfeet might try to spring a surprise attack on us."

"Watch with eyes of hawk," Drags the Rope said, and walked away while motioning for the other warriors to gather around him.

"That man has a way with words," Shakespeare remarked, then coughed violently.

"What does it take to shut you up?" Nate demanded. He went to loosen the shirt.

Shakespeare swatted his friend's hand aside. "I can

undress myself, thank you very much. And I don't understand why you're making such a fuss over such a tiny
bruise.'' He grimaced and sat up.

"Undo your shirt," Nate directed.

"Who appointed you chief?"

"If you don't, I will."

"You're becoming too nasty for your own good,"
Shakespeare groused, but he pulled the bottom hem of
the shirt from under his belt and lifted. "Do you know
anything about doctoring?"

Nate bent closer to inspect the wound. "Once, when
I was in my teens, I found a hurt sparrow and tried to
nurse the bird back to health."

"Tried?"

"It died."

Shakespeare regarded his grinning companion for a
moment, and laughed heartily. "You're learning, son.
You're learning."

"Keep quiet," Nate stated. The pointed tip had ripped
the material and penetrated over an inch into the soft tissue
underneath. No doubt the weakened state of the Blackfoot
had rendered the blow largely ineffectual. Had the warrior
been in prime form, the outcome would have been
drastically different. While blood continued to seep out
and the surrounding flesh was becoming discolored, the
wound did not appear to be life-threatening. "You'll live,"
he mentioned.

"I could have told you that."

"I'll have one of the women dress it for you."

In the act of lowering his shirt, Shakespeare paused and
snorted. "Like hell you will."

"Either one of them does it or I do," Nate informed
him.

Shakespeare opened his mouth, as if about to argue,
then evidently changed his mind and shook his head. "No.

I won't waste my breath. The more I get to know you, the more I find out you're like your Uncle Zeke.''

"I'll take that as a compliment.''

"Yep. Zeke was a hard-headed mule too.'' Shakespeare laughed, grabbed his rifle, and slowly stood. "Give me five minutes and I'll be back in action.''

"Take it easy while we have a breather. As you pointed out, the Blackfeet are bound to be back sooner or later.''

"Likely later.''

"When?''

"My best guess would be right before sunset. If not then, you can expect Mad Dog to hit us at daybreak.''

"Why daybreak?''

"Habit mostly. Indians are partial to surprise attacks at dawn, mainly because villages rarely post guards. Oh, they'll attack at any time if they think they have the edge, but dawn raids are their favorite.''

Nate stared at the forest below, studying the wall of green vegetation that effectively screened their enemies. Were the Blackfeet watching the Shoshones at that very moment and planning their next attack? Most likely.

The layout of the hill favored the defenders. The barren central portion wouldn't hide the approach of a flea, let alone 16 warriors. Only to the south and the north, where the trees flanked the hill, could the Blackfeet draw near to the top without being spotted. Of the two, the south slope presented the greatest threat. The trees came to within 40 feet of the ring of boulders, well within rifle and bow range.

A gurgling whine came from behind Nate, and he turned to find the Shoshones dispatching the injured Blackfeet and taking scalps with unrestrained glee.

Drags the Rope was slicing the hair from a foe whose throat he'd just slit, grinning all the while.

Nate glanced at his companion. "Let's get your wound

tended.'' He walked toward the opening.

"Yep. A natural born leader," Shakespeare said, moving with less than his usual liveliness.

"Oh, please."

"I'm serious. You may turn out to be one of the great ones."

"That blow must have scrambled your brains."

"Scoff if you want, but old William S. put it best," Shakespeare responded. "Why, some are born great, some achieve greatness, and some have greatness thrown upon them. You could wind up in one of those categories."

"I'll settle for just staying alive," Nate said, reentering the fortification. The women and children were still huddled in the center. One of the warriors stood next to a boulder on the southern perimeter, staring at the shadowy, ominous woods.

Winona saw him and beamed happily.

Nate moved over to her. He made the appropriate signs to request that she minister to Shakespeare, and she gladly agreed.

Morning Dew volunteered to help.

"You sure got these womenfolk trained," the frontiersman remarked sarcastically. "And you aren't even part of the family yet."

Nate ignored the barb and gazed overhead at the sun, noting there were at least five hours of daylight remaining, maybe six. Hopefully in that time they could devise a strategy for escaping or defeating the Blackfeet. He glanced down at Black Kettle, and was surprised to discover the warrior's eyes were open and fixed on him. Feeling strangely uncomfortable under such intense scrutiny, he smiled and nodded.

Morning Dew had produced a leather pouch, and she was carefully applying an herbal powder to the mountain man's wound.

Black Kettle addressed Nate, his voice weak, speaking with clear effort.

"Oh, my," Shakespeare said when the warrior concluded.

"What did he say?" Nate inquired, and became aware of both Winona and Morning Dew contemplating him expectantly.

The mountain man chuckled. "He watched you fight the Blackfeet, and he says you truly are a natural-born warrior."

"Thank him for me."

"There's more."

"Oh?"

"Yep. He wants you to marry his daughter," Shakespeare said, and the tone he used indicated he might burst into laughter at any moment.

"I already know that," Nate reminded him.

"Right now," Shakespeare added, and made a choking noise as he suppressed his mirth.

Nate's mouth slackened in shock. He glanced from the frontiersman to the warrior. "Now?"

"Right this minute."

"Out of the question," Nate blurted.

"Give me one good reason."

"I'll give you plenty of reasons. For starters, we're pinned down by a bunch of hostile Blackfeet. They could attack at any minute. This is hardly the ideal time for a wedding."

"You know what they say. There's no time like the present," Shakespeare said good-naturedly.

Becoming angry, Nate glared at the mountain man. "Be serious, for crying out loud."

"I am," Shakespeare stated, and pointed at Black Kettle. "Look at him. Take a good look at him."

Puzzled, Nate grudgingly complied. "So?"

"So what do you see?"

Nate noticed the warrior's ashen complexion and labored breathing and saw blood trickling from the hole made by the lance. He frowned when he answered. "I see a man who is dying."

"Exactly. He knows he doesn't have much time left. Which is why he asked me to ask you to marry his daughter now. He wants to see the two of you hitched before he passes on," Shakespeare said with distinct reverence. "Can you blame him?"

"No," Nate replied softly. He swore he could almost feel Black Kettle's eyes boring into him, as if the warrior was striving to read his mind or plumb the depths of his very soul.

Winona spoke a sentence in Shoshone.

"She says she's ready if you are," Shakespeare translated, grinning. "You certainly can't fault her for being the bashful type."

"I don't know," Nate said hesitantly. He'd already told Black Kettle he would tie the knot, but now that the reality was staring him in the face, as it were, dozens of doubts flooded his mind and caused him to balk. They hardly knew each other. What if they turned out not to be compatible? What if their attraction was only physical? And what if, sometime down the road, he decided he'd made a mistake and elected to return to New York City and Adeline? How could be lead Winona on? Some men might, but it wasn't in his nature. He despised deceit.

Just then Winona went on at some length.

Shakespeare coughed lightly after she concluded and turned a peculiar expression toward his friend. "Well, Nathaniel, she said a mouthful. If you've changed your mind, she says she understands. She knows how hard marriages can be between Indians and whites, and she knows that many whites look down their noses at her people. She wouldn't want to be a burden to you. So there's no hard feelings on her part if you want to call it off, no matter what you may have promised her father.''

Nate looked at Winona and was flabbergasted to observe fear in her lovely eyes, fear inspired by his possible refusal, fear that her heart would be crushed by the man to whom she had so openly and unconditionally given herself. Fear of him. The very last emotion he would ever want her to feel because of him. Before he even quite knew what he was doing, he had taken a step and tenderly caressed her cheek. ''Tell her I'm a man of my word. I'll be her husband if she wants me.''

Speaking in an unusually gravelly tone, Shakespeare relayed the message.

Conspicuous relief mellowed Winona's features and she clasped Nate's hand in her own.

''But I still don't see how we can get married here,'' Nate commented absently. ''Don't we need a preacher to make it nice and legal?''

Shakespeare snorted. ''There is no law west of the Mississippi. None that counts anyway. And as far as the ceremony goes, what were you expecting? A formal gown and organ music?''

''No,'' Nate said sheepishly.

''You'll get hitched Indian fashion, and even then you won't have the full affair,'' Shakespeare stated. He began tucking his shirt under his belt. ''You stay put. I'll tend to the preparations.'' He hurried off, chuckling and muttering under his breath.

Nate stood next to Winona, at a loss for words, slightly dazed by the precipitous turn of events. He must be dreaming. Was he really about to tie the knot? To an Indian woman, no less? Was he in his right mind or had the sequence of harrowing experiences since he'd left St. Louis rattled his noggin?

The word spread quickly among the Shoshones. Drags the Rope and the other warriors, having finished taking scalps, took up guard positions around the rim. The women and children gathered near Black Kettle's travois to witness the event, many whispering and giggling. And every one of them stared openly at the groom.

Nate felt as if he were under a microscope.

Shakespeare, adopting a solemn air belied by the way the corners of his mouth continually curled upward, stood to the right of the travois and had the couple stand in front of Black Kettle. "Are you ready?" he asked Nate.

"Why do I feel like heading for the hills?"

"You're already *on* a hill, and you evaded the question. Are you ready?"

"Is a man ever ready for marriage?"

"Now's not the time to wax philosophical. Are you ready or not, damn it?"

Nate inhaled deeply and nodded. "Ready."

"Good." Shakespeare addressed Black Kettle, who had managed to prop himself on his elbows. The warrior then relayed a series of queries through the frontiersman. "Do you want to take Winona as your wife?"

"You know I do."

"Do you promise to protect her, to treat her kindly, to stay with her in good times and bad?"

"Yes," Nate said.

"Do you primise to carry on the line by having as many sons as you can?"

"I'll do my best," Nate pledged.

"What do you offer to buy her with?"

Nate blinked and straightened in consternation. "Buy her? No one said anything about buying her."

"Remember what I told you about how Indian men purchase their brides? Normally, Black Kettle would receive about six horses for a pretty thing like Winona.

But this is a special case. Still, you have to offer something. What will it be?''

"I don't have six horses," Nate said. "All I have is my pack horse."

"Done," Shakespeare stated, and conveyed the news to Black Kettle.

"Wait a minute!" Nate exclaimed. "I didn't mean—"

"Too late," Shakespeare interrupted. "He accepts. Congratulations. You're now husband and wife."

Stunned, Nate looked at his bride, who was standing coyly with her head bowed. "What? Just like that? You're joking."

"Nope," Shakespeare said, and grasped his friend's right hand in a firm shake. "Let me be the first one to offer my condolences."

"Condolences?"

"I've been married before, if you'll recollect."

Peeved, Nate tore his hand free and gestured to Winona. "And what about her? Doesn't she take part in the vows?"

"What vows? You gave Black Kettle your horse. She's yours. It's as simple as that."

"But—"

"It's too late to change your mind," Shakespeare commented, his eyes twinkling. "You're hitched."

"But—"

"And I'm sorry to say that you don't even get to kiss the bride. The Shoshones don't go in for public displays of affection. So save your puckering for when you're alone."

"There has to be more to it than this!" Nate exploded.

"Well, if you want to be a stickler for formality, there's usually a big feast to celebrate. But under the circumstances, I reckon it's best if we hold off on the festivities. Don't you agree?"

Nate nodded blankly. His thoughts were whirling at a

cyclonic rate, yet his body was functioning in slow motion. He gazed at his bride in a dreamlike state, viewing her as an unreal vision of beauty and charm.

The next instant a strident scream brought him back to reality with a vengeance.

One of the Shoshone women staggered forward and stumbled, sinking to her knees, her torso pierced by an arrow, the bloody point jutting from between her breasts.

Chapter Eighteen

For a minute panic prevailed.

Everyone scrambled for cover, dashing for the shelter of the boulders. The woman who had been shot was supported by three others and half-carried to the slabs alongside the spring. At Morning Dew's urging, Shakespeare and Nate lifted Black Kettle from the platform and placed him at the base of the boulders. One of the warriors stationed along the southern perimeter began shouting excitedly, and all of the Shoshone men converged on him.

"Let's go," Shakespeare said, and hurried toward them.

Nate glanced at Winona, regretting they had married under such hazardous circumstances and wishing he could take her in his arms to express his affection. Instead, he gave her arm a tender squeeze and raced after the frontiersman.

Drags the Rope was peering at the forest below. He looked around and scowled. "Red Knife see Blackfeet there," he stated, and pointed at a point in the trees 50 feet from the rim.

"The bastards are going to pick us off," Shakespeare declared angrily. "They'll try and soften us up for their attack.''

As if in confirmation, a warrior yelled and jabbed his finger skyward.

Nate looked up in time to see the sunlight glinting off an arrow as the shaft arced high in the air and streaked down at the enclosed area on the summit.

Drags the Rope cried out a warning.

All eyes swung upward. The arrow descended in the center, missing the Shoshones huddled beside the rocks by a wide margin, but the tip still found a target. Purely by chance the arrow struck one of the horses, smacking into the animal's neck and burying itself to the feathers. The horse, neighing in torment and terror, scrambled erect and bolted for the eastern opening.

Several of the warriors endeavored to head the animal off, without success.

Snorting and whinnying, the horse galloped between the boulders and fled down the east slope.

''Damn their stinking bones!'' Shakespeare fumed, and brazenly stood to his full height so he could shake his left fist at the trees and curse the Blackfeet mightily.

''Get down!'' Nate snapped, grabbing the older man's leflt arm and hauling him safely behind the slab. ''What are you trying to do? Get yourself killed?''

A fit of coughing struck the frontiersman and he doubled over, his arms pressed against his left side. In a minute the paroxysm subsided and he leaned on the boulder. ''Whew! I'm not as spry as I used to be.''

''Not fifteen minutes ago you were bashed by a war club.''

''What's that got to do with anything? If you stay out here long enough, you learn to shrug those things off.''

''You're impossible,'' Nate mumbled, and scanned their immediate surroundings. The animals herded together in the middle were in grave peril, as were the Shoshones crouched behind boulders on the west, north, and east sides of the clearing, which included Winona and her family. "We have to get everyone on the south side," he stated urgently.

Drags the Rope nodded in agreement and started yelling for his people to move to safety.

"I'll be right back," Nate said. He propped the Hawken against a rock slab and sprinted toward his new in-laws. Halfway across the open track he heard Shakespeare voice a shout of alarm.

"Another arrow! Look out!"

Nate twisted and saw the incoming shaft, its metal point gleaming, on its downward sweep. He automatically calculated the trajectory, and in a flash perceived that one of the horses would be hit. He darted to his left, intending to pull the animal onto its feet and remove it from harm's way, but compared to a streaking arrow his speed was equivalent to that of a tortoise.

The Blackfoot shaft smacked into the brown stallion high on the animal's forehead, thrusting through skin, flesh, and even bone, drilling through to the cranial cavity and skewering the hapless horse's brain. It stiffened, opened its mouth, then convulsed silently for half a minute. Finally, its eyes rolling in their sockets, the stallion simply keeled over, blood and froth bubbling over its lips.

Nate didn't waste any more time on the animal. More arrows would be forthcoming. He sprinted to the north where Winona and Morning Dew were already turning the horse hauling the travois. Black Kettle had reclined on his back once again, exhausted by the energy he had expended during the wedding ceremony. "Let me," Nate said, and signed his desire to lead the horse. He grabbed the reins and headed to the south.

Winona and Morning Dew stepped to the travois, each on a different side, prepared to aid Black Kettle if needed.

The rest of the band was flocking to the boulders on the southern perimeter.

But what about the horses? Nate wondered as he hastened along. There was nowhere to shelter the mounts and the dogs from the rain of deadly missiles. So far the Blackfeet had fired a few shafts; soon they would unleash a dozen bolts at a time. The horses and dogs would be easy pickings. Mulling the predicament, he led the travois animal to within 15 feet of relative safety when Shakespeare yelled again.

"More arrows! Lots of them!"

Nate looked up, his breath catching in his throat at the sight of nine or ten shafts cleaving the air above the summit. Several were directly overhead. Spinning, he dashed to Black Kettle and hooked his left arm under the warrior's shoulder.

Winona and Morning Dew stepped in to help.

Resembling the spattering of heavy hail, the arrows thudded home. Many impaled victims. One found Morning Dew.

Nate would never forget the image of the shaft striking his mother-in-law on the left shoulder and protruding out her dress in the vicinity of her navel. He was staring into her eyes when she took the arrow, and he saw a flicker of exquisite anguish promptly replaced by something else—sorrow, he thought—and she collapsed.

Winona screamed and moved to her mother's side.

"There's nothing we can do for her," Nate said, but his words were meaningless to his wife and he couldn't execute sign language while holding Black Kettle in his arms. The warrior stared at his mate in silent horror.

Pandemonium reigned on the hill. Six Shoshones were down, dead or dying, and two women were screeching in the throes of agony. Injured horses were up and running wildly in circles, spooking other animals. And in the midst of the bedlam other Shoshones were trying to reach the south side before another volley descended.

"We've got to get out of the open," Nate told Winona. She leaned over her mother, oblivious to the world. He took a step and was about to snatch at her hair when a friendly voice sounded to his right.

"Let me take Black Kettle, Nate. You bring the missus."

Nate glanced at his friend. "Are you sure you're up to it?"

"Do you want to argue or become a porcupine?" Shakespeare countered, and grasped the warrior under the arms.

Inexpressibly grateful, Nate crouched next to Winona and placed his hands on her shoulders. "Come on," he urged. "Please."

She sobbed, tears flowing down her full cheeks.

"Hurry," Nate said, and tried to lift her. He glanced upward and felt a tingle run along his spine as he beheld yet another shower of shafts flying from the forest. His mind shrieked for him to move, and move he did, forcibly yanking Winona upright and propelling her toward the sheltering boulders. She meekly submitted to the leading. In five leaping strides he got them within reach of the perimeter, and he threw himself forward the last few yards, carrying her with him.

The volley thudded down. Four more Shoshones were hit, and three horses. One of the dogs was lanced clear through and fell without so much as a whimper.

Nate rose to his knees, pulling Winona with him.

Black Kettle rested with his back to the nearest boulder, his eyes still locked on Morning Dew, the smallest spark of vitality flickering in his sorrowful eyes.

"Those dirty vermin!" Shakespeare barked, surveying the slaughter.

Almost all of the Shoshones still alive had reached the haven of the southern rim. A few slow ones, the injured, were being assisted by others. Two horses took off down the east slope.

Drags the Rope and several warriors were firing arrows wildly at the forest.

"Save your shafts," Nate advised. "You'll need them."

The young warrior turned a visage full of rage and hatred toward the two white men. "Mad Dog's heart mine!" he growled.

"You may have to wait your turn," Nate said, gazing at Morning Dew.

"We need a plan," Shakespeare said, stating the obvious, and peeked over the boulder in front of him. "Damn! More arrows!"

Nate saw them too. Only four shafts this time, and miraculously each missed. He braced for others, but five minutes elapsed uneventfully.

"We can't make a run for it," Shakespeare remarked. "There aren't enough horses for everyone, and we'd be picked off before we covered a hundred yards."

"Charge trees then," Drags the Rope proposed.

"And commit suicide? No, thanks," Shakespeare replied. "We'd be lucky if any of us made it to the woods. And then what do you think would happen to the women and children? They'd be at the mercy of Mad Dog, and we both know what that son of a bitch would do to them."

Drags the Rope grunted.

The frontiersman swiveled toward Nate. "What about you? Have any brilliant ideas?"

"No."

"We've got to—" Shakespeare began, and looked skyward. "More arrows!" he announced.

Four slim missiles streaked out of the blue and plunged into the earth in the middle of the enclosed space. The remaining horses and dogs were milling near the spring, and they escaped being struck.

The mountain man cackled. "That's four more those buzzards have wasted."

Nate's forehead creased in contemplation. Once again the Blackfeet had fired only four shafts. Why? Were they conserving their arrows for their main assault?

"I propose we stick it out here until dark, then slip away," Shakespeare stated. "They can't hit us behind these boulders, so we're safe for the time being."

"I suppose," Nate said, bothered by a vague sensation of unease, his intuition telling him that there was an aspect to the battle he was overlooking. Something was not right, but he couldn't put his finger on it.

"Yes, sir," Shakespeare went on enthusiastically. "Even if the Blackfeet do post sentries around this hill, we can fight our way out and cover the women and youngsters."

"Women, children fight," Drags the Rope declared.

"I know they can," Shakespeare acknowledged. "Shoshone women are known for their courage."

Nate glanced at his wife, who had rested her head on her father's left shoulder and now weeped soundlessly. He wanted to embrace her, to soothe her, and he started to lift his right arm when Shakespeare uttered a remark that inexplicably troubled him immensely.

"If those mangy Blackfeet try to sneak up on us, we'll hear them. There's a lot of loose rock to give them away. We'll have to watch out for the same stuff when we cut out."

The frontiersman had a point. Nate recalled seeing the loose rock on the east and west side of the hill. But he hadn't noticed any to the south, where the Blackfeet were currently congregated, or to the north.

The north!

A cold wind seemed to tingle Nate's skin as he looked at the boulders on the north side of the summit. The arrows had driven all of the Shoshones away from those boulders, which overlooked the trees that came within 60 feet of the rim, leaving the north slope undefended, providing an undisputed approach route for the enemy.

What if forcing the defenders away from the north side had been a deliberate stratagem?

What if the Blackfeet were cleverer than anyone gave them credit for being?

What if Mad Dog had no intention of waiting until tomorrow morning to launch the attack? What if he wasn't even going to wait until sunset?

Why had the number of arrows drastically fallen off? And why had there been that five-minute span when no shafts were fired? What had the Blackfeet been doing during those five minutes?

"Shakespeare," Nate said softly, scanning the northern perimeter, filled with an equal measure of dread and doubt, wondering if perhaps he might be wrong, might be worried over nothing. He noticed his friend conversing with Drags the Rope, and realized the mountain man hadn't heard him. Instinctively he reached for his Hawken, and as he did he recalled the sage advice Shakespeare had dispensed after the incident with the Utes. "You should always trust your own instincts, no matter what someone else with more experience might tell you. Go with the gut, as I like to say." Well, his gut was telling him that they were in imminent danger, terrible danger, so he spoke louder and urgently. "Shakespeare!"

The frontiersman looked at him anxiously, alerted by his tone. "What is it?"

"The north rim—" Nate started to say, and then he saw them, saw the Blackfeet sweeping over and around the boulders to the north at the same moment they vented ear-splitting war whoops. He whipped up his rifle, snapped off a shot, and was gratified to see a Blackfoot drop.

A fraction of a second later Shakespeare's rifle cracked and a second attacker pitched onto his face.

The two shots, booming almost at the very instant they appeared, gave the Blackfeet brief pause as they ducked for cover or crouched to avoid being the next target. They had expected to take the defenders totally unawares, and they were collectively surprised that resistance should be so swift and lethal.

The two shots had another effect. By causing the Blackfeet to briefly check their rush, even for the short span of a few seconds, the Shoshones were given time to react to the startling discovery they were outflanked. The warriors gave tongue to soul-stirring challenges of their own, and charged.

Nate frantically reloaded his rifle and glimpsed Shakespeare doing the same.

Winona moved in front of her father, fury contorting her features, her fists clenched, prepared to defend his life with her own.

A fierce desperation pervaded the Shoshone warriors. Drags the Rope and the others were outnumbered, but they were fighting for the lives of their loved ones, for the very survival of their band, and such knowledge lent an inhuman savagery to their struggle. They unleashed a volley of their own, slaying six of their adversaries, and then closed in personal mortal combat.

Nate was raising the Hawken again when he realized very few of the Blackfeet carried rifles or bows. Most were armed with war clubs, tomahawks, and knifes, weapons best employed in close-in battle. Why hadn't they brought their fusees and bows and easily finished off the Shoshones? Nate asked himself. He percieved the answer as he took aim on a burly Blackfoot who had just stabbed a Shoshone warrior. Coup. The Blackfeet wanted to count the highest possible coup, and to do so they must engage the Shoshones man to man. Well, they could count all the coup they wanted. His main concern was staying alive. He squeezed the trigger, his ball catching the Blackfoot in the forehead and catapulting the man to the ground.

Now the center of the open track was a swirling melee of yelling and screaming Indians. Knives flashed. Clubs swung right and left. Tomahawks cleaved the air.

Nate saw Drags the Rope using a knife to hold off three foes. He leaned the rifle against the boulder, drew one of his pistols and gave it to Winona, then raced toward the conflict, drawing his other pistol. The confusing whirl of forms prevented him from determining which side was winning, although the Shoshones appeared to be holding their own. He came within ten feet of Drags the Rope, halted, and sighted on a Blackfoot swinging a club. His shot struck the warrior in the left cheek, spinning the man around and dropping him in his tracks.

A tall, screeching Blackfoot wearing buckskins and a dark hat ran directly at Nate, a tomahawk in his right hand.

There wasn't time to reload the pistol. Nate grasped his own tomahawk and tensed to meet the rush. He blocked a powerful swipe that would have split his skull wide open, then slashed at the warrior's midsection.

The Blackfoot skillfully danced aside and swung again.

Nate parried that blow, then another and another, put on the defensive by the warrior's adroit, unflagging onslaught. He retreated, the empty pistol still clutched in his left hand. A reverse thrust almost caught him in the neck, and he darted to the right.

The Blackfoot glanced down, then did a strange thing. He smiled. And lunged, his hat falling off in the process.

Stepping backwards, perplexed by the enigmatic glance, Nate apprehended its significance a heartbeat later when the heel of his right foot connected with a rock, throwing him off balance, and he fell.

Whooping triumphantly, the Blackfoot took a stride and raised his tomahawk for the death blow.

Flat on his back, his arms outflung, Nate stiffened in anticipation of the warrior's tomahawk slicing into his flesh. The glinting edge hung suspended in the air for a moment, and suddenly, incredibly, the Blackfoot looked up, looking at something or someone beyond Nate's line of vision.

Feral hatred etched the warrior's countenance, and he made a motion as if about to throw the tomahawk.

A shot rang out.

The Blackfoot's right eye was blown apart by the ball that penetrated his head and ruptured out the rear, showering hair, skin, and gore on the ground. His arms sagged, he swayed, and toppled over to the left.

Nate scrambled erect and turned, thinking he would find Shakespeare standing behind him. Instead, much to his astonishment, he discovered Black Kettle.

A pale shadow of his former self, a smoking pistol clutched in both hands, the leader of the band mustered a broad smile, cast a benign, almost grateful gaze at Nate, and sank slowly to his knees.

Heedless of his own safety, Nate bounded to Black Kettle's side. He recognized the pistol as his own and realized Winona had given the weapon to her father.

Winona!

Where was she?

Nate scanned the summit and recieved a shock. Eleven Shoshone women had entered the fray armed with knives, stones, and whatever else they could get their hands on. Five Shoshone boys, each between eight and 14 years of age, had also gone to the aid of the warriors. The Blackfeet were battling furiously, but now they were the ones who were outnumbered, and they were learning the hard way that a knife in the hands of an enraged woman or boy was every bit as deadly as a blade wielded by a man. The very existence of the Shoshone band was at stake, and every able-bodied member had rallied to the cause.

A figure materialized on Nate's right and he rotated, thinking it might be a Blackfoot.

Winona squatted next to her father, her countenance a mask of sadness.

Concerned that one of the Blackfeet might bear down on them, Nate quickly reloaded both pistols. As he took the one gun from Black Kettle, his father-in-law stared into his eyes and spoke a single word.

A tremendous cry of exultation shook the heavens.

Nate stood, both arms extended, but his further participation proved to be unnecessary.

Nine Blackfeet were dead, sprawled on the ground in spreading pools of their own blood, most bearing multiple wounds. The rest of the attackers had fled, barely escaping with their lives, clambering over the boulders or fleeing through the gaps as fast as their legs would carry them.

The carnage was appalling. Shoshone bodies dotted the enclosed area. Only five warriors were still standing, including Drags the Rope, and he had sustained a wicked gash on the right side of his chest. Most of the other warriors were also injured, but not as extensively, and many of the women bore cuts or bruises or both.

"We did it."

Nate turned to his left at the subdued words. There stood Shakespeare, his shoulders slumped, his face caked with sweat and dust. "Do you think the Blackfeet are gone for good?"

The frontiersman nodded wearily. "They took quite a licking. The bastards won't have anything to celebrate when they return to their village." He gazed at the

Blackfoot slain by Black Kettle. "Did you do this?"

"No. Black Kettle did."

"Well, I reckon he won't mind," Shakespeare said, and stepped to the dark hat lying in the dirt. He picked it up, smacked the fur against his leg a few times, and extended his arm to Nate. "Here. I don't like to see a good hat go to waste and I already have one."

"I don't need it."

"You will come winter," Shakespeare told him. "Don't argue. Black Kettle has no use for it. And he'd want you to have Mad Dog's hat."

"Mad Dog's?" Nate repeated in surprise. He took the handcrafted headgear in his right hand, feeling the soft texture of the fur. "Maybe Black Kettle would like to have this," he stated, and pivoted to offer the trophy to his father-in-law. Not until then did he understand Shakespeare's comment.

Winona was on her knees, her hands clasped under her chin, her eyes filled with tears. On his back in front of her, his eyes open but lifeless, his profile reflecting an attitude of profound peace, lay Black Kettle.

Epilogue

"You didn't make out so bad."

Nate looked to his right at his friend, frowning at the callousness of the comment, then stared straight ahead at the valley before them. He tightened his grip on the mare's reins and spoke sarcastically. "No, I didn't make out too bad. Both my wife's mother and father were killed, but other than that everything is just terrific."

"That isn't what I meant and you know it," Shakespeare countered. "I miss them more than you ever will. They were my close friends, remember?"

A twinge of guilt tweaked Nate's conscience. "Sorry. I guess I'm just taking out my frustration on you."

"Now that you're married, you're not supposed to get testy with your friends," Shakespeare noted, grinning impishly. "What do you think you have a wife for?"

"I'm beginning to wonder."

"Has anyone ever told you that you take life too seriously?" Shakespeare asked.

"I take life the only way I know how."

The rode in silence for a minute.

The frontiersman coughed lightly. "Actually, I was

referring to that fact that you received two of the horses the Blackfeet left behind. Now you have enough for your woman and all your goods.''

"Yes," Nate said dryly.

Shakepeare hissed in exasperation. "I had no idea you can be so grumpy."

"I have my reason," Nate stated obstinately. He shifted in the saddle and gazed back at the line of Shoshones trailing them, studiously refraining from looking at his wife, who was riding on a black gelding not two yards to his rear.

"Are you going to mope like this all the way to the rendezvous?" the mountain man asked.

"I may," Nate said, facing front again.

"You're worse than a kid, you know that?"

Nate's anger got the better of him and he whirled on his friend. "Damn it! She should have listened to me!"

A smile creased Shakespeare's mouth. "Since when are wives supposed to listen to their husbands? You have a lot to learn about marriage. When a woman agrees to hitch herself to a man, she's not agreeing to do every little thing he wants. She reserves the right to disagree, and disagree she will. Every chance she gets. Sometimes I think women aren't satisfied unless they can bicker about an issue first.'' He paused and chuckled. "Of course, they usually wind up doing what they want to anyway. Nine times out of ten a woman will outthink a man. Always remember that."

"You're a big help."

"I'm not done yet. I'm not suggesting you roll over and give in to your wife every time you have a spat. You can't be weak. A woman never respects a weakling. She'll pout and be bitchy and quarrel for the dumbest reasons in Creation, but through it all she expects her man to be strong,'' Shakespeare stated, and shook his head in amazement. "Never did make much sense to me. They marry the strongest man they can find, then they get all hot under the collar when he stands by his own guns.''

"I'll be sure and write down your words of wisdom for posterity," Nate cracked.

"It's nice to see you can still make a joke."

Nate sighed and glanced at his friend. "Do you think I'm in the wrong?"

"Who's to judge? I do know she can't understand why you're so upset. To her it's the normal course of things. It's like eating and sleeping. Just has to be done."

"What have I gotten myself into?" Nate queried rhetorically.

"Ain't love grand?" Shakespeare responded, beaming.

"Love," Nate repeated softly, still immensely disturbed. But he did love her. That was the whole problem. He loved her so much, cared for her with all of his heart and soul, and he couldn't bear the thought of her being harmed in any way. Especially when he possessed the power to prevent it. And he'd tried. He'd really tried. Unfortunately, he couldn't keep his eyes on her 24 hours a day.

"We should be at the rendezvous in three hours," Shakespeare mentioned.

Nate nodded, then slowed the mare so his wife could ride alongside him. He smiled and stared at her, feasting his eyes on her loveliness.

Winona eagerly returned the smile.

Straining his self-control to the limit, Nate forced himself to keep smiling as his gaze drifted lower until he was looking at the strip of hide wrapped around her left hand, the hide that served as a bandage, the hide she had secured to staunch the flow of her blood after she chopped the tips off two of her fingers.

What *had* he gotten himself into?

Only time would tell.